th

FAIR,
baby

K WEBSTER

To my **HUSBAND**,

Thank you for teaching me that life's not **FAIR**...
and that's what makes you try harder.

I **LOVE** you, hunny bunny.

War and Peace Series Reading Order

"The very essence of romance is uncertainty."

—Oscar Wilde, *The Importance of Being Earnest and Other Plays*

Warning:

This Isn't Fair, Baby is a dark romance. Extreme sexual themes and violence, which could trigger emotional distress, are found in this story. If you are sensitive to dark themes, then this story is not for you. *This Isn't Fair, Baby* is the sixth book in the series. Please read the first five books before reading this one to fully understand the story.

PART ONE:

"Everybody Wants to Rule the World" by Lorde

PROLOGUE | Vee

Five years old...

THIS HOUSE IS PRETTY. LIKE THE CASTLE IN MY *BEAUTY and the Beast* movie. There are so many rooms to play hide-and-seek in. I wish Mommy would play with me. She never does, though.

Once I've looked inside every room in the castle, I run down the long hallway toward Mommy's and Daddy's room. We're on a vacation, Daddy told me. A work vacation. All I know is we're not in California anymore. We got on an airplane and flew far, far away to this castle.

"Mommy!" I call out. "Where are you?"

Maybe she is playing a game with me. The thought makes my heart thump in my chest. When I get close to her room, I can hear the music playing inside. And as I round the corner, I see her dancing.

Mommy is so pretty with her shiny red hair, which looks like it has gold strands in it sometimes. Like the mermaid in my favorite Disney movie. Her eyes even sparkle every now and again. I love when they sparkle because that means she's in a good mood. When she's in a bad mood, she makes me go play by myself.

I let out a squeal and drop my backpack full of toys and coloring books. I start dancing in circles and love the way my dress flares out around me. I'm a princess like Mommy.

"Dancing! Dancing!" I cheer out in delight.

As if my words make her angry, she stops dancing and turns to stare at me. Some white powder is on her nose and her green eyes look almost black. Her smile is gone. She bares her teeth at me and her lip curls up as if she's grossed out by me.

"I thought I told you to go play," she snaps and then sniffs, like she has a cold.

"But I thought we were dancing, Mom—"

"For crying out loud, Vienna! Mommy has to test Daddy's merchandise. I can't do that with you bothering me. Go play," she spits out and rubs at her nose.

"But Daddy said to stay inside and—"

"Now!"

Her harsh words used to make me cry, but I'm used to them now. Nothing makes me cry. Daddy says I'm fierce… like a dragon. I always smile when he says that, yet deep down I wish I were fierce, but also a princess. Why can't I be pretty and breathe fire at the same time?

Mommy's hand swats at me, and I scamper away from her. I scoop up my backpack along the way out the door. Eager to explore, I run along the narrow hallways until I find one that leads outside. As soon as I push through the door, the summer heat cloaks me like my warm blanket back home.

Even though Daddy told me to stay inside, I listen to Mommy's instructions and start exploring the outside of the castle. Daddy has taken us on lots of vacations to Colombia, but this is the first time we've visited this castle.

I'm humming a song when I hear voices. Shouting. Curiosity gets the best of me, and I sneak around the side of the stone wall to see what all the commotion is about. A man with big muscles and a scary smile is holding a huge knife. He's teasing someone, but I can't see who. I sneak over to a rose bush and crouch behind it. The roses are big and red, kind of like the ones in my *Beauty and the Beast* movie. I want to pick one but I know roses have thorns. Instead, I lean in and inhale the sweet scent.

"You'll pay for this," the scary man growls, stealing my attention away from the roses. His big knife gleams in the bright sunlight.

I peek around the bush to get a better look. Finally, I see who the scary man is yelling at. A skinny boy is sprawled out on the grass with his hands up, like he's afraid the man will hurt him. Sometimes I hold my hands up like that when Mommy is mad. She doesn't hit me often, but her eyes can be mean. I always worry she will.

"No me robé ningúna cocaína," the boy says, his voice shaking. I don't know what he's saying, but it sounds like he's trying to make the scary man understand.

"Te cojì con el producto en tu bolsa. Ahora vas a pagar con tu vida. Nadie le falta el respeto a mi familia," the scary man hisses. I half expect him to change into a monster right under the hot, sunny rays. Kind of like when Beast turns into a human. But backward and scarier.

"Por favor, señor." The boy seems sad and afraid. I wish

I could yell at the scary man to stop waving his knife at him.

While they continue to argue, I slide my backpack off and dig around. I don't have a real knife but I have a yellow plastic one I use to cut my Play-Doh. Once I have it in my tiny grip, I rise from behind the bush. I watch in awe for a moment as the scary man moves his arm fast and fancy, like he's a dancer but with just one arm. It's almost magical. Until I see the blood covering his white button-down shirt, like the ones Daddy wears.

"No!" I cry out from my hiding spot.

The scary man freezes and turns, his eyes locking onto mine. "Run along, child." His accent is thick, but I understand his words this time. "Run to your father." He breaks our stare to glare down at the bloody boy, who doesn't move. When he holds the knife up like he might stab him, I charge for the scary man.

"Noooooo!" I screech and hold my yellow knife up as I run.

The scary man laughs—loud and too cold for this hot day—as I try to stab him with my weapon. He snorts before easily pushing me to the grass beside the boy.

"Hijos de puta," he grumbles and shakes his head before stalking off.

I turn to regard the boy. His face is covered in blood. The dirty white T-shirt he's wearing is now torn and bright red, like the roses on the bush. He's bleeding everywhere. When he lifts a shaking hand that drips with blood, I let out a small shriek. But he smiles through his pain.

"Un ángel. Me estoy muriendo y tu eres mi ángel." His voice is deep like Daddy's. I can tell he's older like my cousin Seth who can drive.

"Shh," I coo to the boy. His lip wobbles and he looks lost. I can't see his eyes because they're squinted shut against the bright sunshine. "I have Band-Aids," I assure him. "They're *Toy Story,* so boys can like them too."

Tears streak down his cheeks and gurgling sounds escape him. The sounds scare me, but I can fix him. With newfound determination, I run back to the bush to grab my backpack. Once I snag it up, I rush back to my patient. He's quiet as I pull out my box of Band-Aids and carefully peel apart each one. The box was nearly full—Daddy bought it for me at the airport when we arrived in Colombia after I fell and skinned my knee—so I'm able to put them all over his bloody face. With Buzz Lightyear and Woody staring back at me with big smiles on their faces, I believe this boy will get better.

"¡Llama ayuda, hermano!" a boy shouts from somewhere behind us.

I turn to see an older boy with messy black hair running toward me. He doesn't seem scary like the man from before. In fact, he looks like he might cry.

"I fixed him," I assure the boy when he kneels beside me. "He's going to get all better now." I go to pat him, but he stares at my bloody hand as though he's afraid it will bite him. *Hands don't bite, silly.*

His eyes that are almost purple in the sunlight shimmer with tears. "Please go inside, little girl." He points at the house. "My little brother is in the kitchen. Have him help you clean up." I like this boy's accent.

I reach into my bag and tug out Mr. Snuffles, my new stuffed cat, which Daddy bought me in a gift shop before we came to the castle. Mr. Snuffles won't miss me. Besides, this bloody boy needs him more than I do. I'll just ask Daddy to buy me a new one.

"Here you go," I tell the bloody boy, who seems to have fallen asleep. "Mr. Snuffles wants to stay with you." I lift his messy arm and stuff the cat in the crook of it.

The purple-eyed boy beside me starts to cry. "I think he's dead."

I ignore the sad boy and give the bloody boy a hug good-bye. Then, I scoop up my backpack and walk slowly back to the castle. When I reach the doorway, I turn and look at the bloody boy and the sad boy. One sobs loudly. The other doesn't make a peep.

He's going to be okay.

I fixed him.

With a smile, I turn and run right into another boy. This boy looks to be my same age. This boy has the prettiest dark brown eyes I've ever seen.

"Hi," I wave a bloody hand at him and grin. "I'm Vee. Can we be friends?"

His eyes widen but he nods slowly. A small smile creeps on his face. "We can be friends if you can catch me." He gives me a tiny shove before turning and running away. Fast. My new friend is super fast.

But I'll catch him.

Tossing my backpack to the floor, I chase after him.

I | Vee

Present

"WAKE UP, DIABLA ROJA," A DEEP VOICE RUMBLES AS IT parts its way through the fog clouding my mind.

I blink away the confusion and take in the eyes before me. Dark brown. Piercing. Calculating. Esteban.

"Morning."

He's not smiling, though. And while that's not uncommon for Esteban, I sense something is wrong.

"We need to discuss a few things," he bites out. When I stare at him with a frown for a second too long, his palm cracks across my thigh. "¡Levantate!"

My flesh stings, but I jolt into action. The last thing I want is Esteban angry with me. I don't want to see that fury flickering in his eyes, like the night he took my mother and I from her house after I witnessed the death of my father. That night he was furious and roaring about revenge and what was owed to him.

He stole me.

And my mother.

Our families were joined by business, and I'd always hoped they'd be by matrimony one day as well.

But nothing went as planned. Everything was destroyed.

"Whatever it is that's going on in your head, I want it gone," Esteban snaps as he snags my wrist in his brutal grip.

My heart rate skitters in my chest, and I clumsily follow after him. He's fully dressed in a pair of slacks and a white button-down shirt that fits his muscled body like a glove. I, on the other hand, am dressed exactly how he likes me. Which is not dressed at all.

"Sit," he commands and points to the floor in front of a chair in the small living room.

I nod and fall to my knees. My head starts to throb much like it always does these days. I'm sure it's because I always feel so hungry. Maybe today he'll feed me more than just a sandwich. He takes a seat in the chair and gently grabs my throat to pull me between his thighs. I look up at him with wide eyes as my palms caress his knees through his slacks.

"What did I do wrong?" My voice is but a whisper, but I know he hears me. Esteban never misses a thing. Not when it comes to me. That's one thing I can say about him. I'm his entire focus. I've never been anyone's entire focus before.

His hard gaze softens as he leans forward. A large palm strokes the side of my head, and I lean against it. My eyes flutter closed as I relish his gentle touch.

"Look at me," he murmurs, his fingers twisting into my hair.

I pop my eyes back open and fixate on his mouth. Just thinking about where his mouth was last night sends a ripple of need coursing through me. He may not drug me like he did my mother, but I'm completely addicted to him. It's his touch I need. His dark eyes roaming over my body. The deep rumble of his voice quaking down to my very soul.

I've never felt so consumed before. Not even by Oscar.

My heart rate quickens at the thought of his name. Thinking about Ozzy confuses me. Several days ago, Esteban spoke to him over the phone. He said he'd be coming out to meet with us. I wonder if all connection with Oscar has been severed. If I'll ever feel about him the way I seem to feel about Esteban. My mind can't comprehend turning off all of these feelings for Esteban in the blink of an eye and switching back on how I felt for Oscar. Everything is hazy and all messed up. If I could just get rid of this headache, maybe I could think clearly.

A sharp slap to my face stuns me, and I clutch my stinging flesh. The throb in my head intensifies. I dart my eyes up to Esteban's which are blazing with fury.

"We spent so many months teaching you how to behave. Who you belong to. And for what? For you to forget it the moment I take you out of your metal prison? Do we need to go back and start over?" he hisses, the brutal grip on my hair tightening.

I start to shake my head but I can't move it. Swallowing, I force out my words. "N-No. I'm just tired, I think. Hungry." While it's technically a lie about where my thoughts have been, I am tired and hungry. Ever since leaving the container, I can't help but feel starved all the time. Esteban brings me my meals. Esteban feeds me. But it never feels like enough. And everything seems foggy—as if Esteban is the lighthouse beaconing for me. Everything around me feels like a blur.

"You can eat later," he hisses. "We need to talk about tonight."

I try not to fixate on the way his nostrils flare with anger. Sometimes they flare when his face is between my thighs as he inhales me. Sometimes they flare when he grabs me by the throat and pins me to the bed.

Focus, Vee.

"You belong to me," he bites out, and his grip in my hair loosens. He goes back to petting the side of my head, like I'm his dog. "Whatever childhood fantasies you had of growing up to marry my little brother are over. At one time, our families would have supported that. Now that it's just the three of us left, everything will play out differently."

My gaze falls to his lips. I wonder if he's eaten anything today.

"Do you understand, Roja?"

Upon hearing the pet name he coined for me, my mind flashes to several days ago when I was his prisoner, trapped in a metal container he'd kept me in for months. When he'd left to try and steal Brie, so I'd have a friend. It ended up nearly getting him killed in the process. As a result, my mother died from heroin withdrawals, and I was on the brink of starvation. But he came back. He came back and plucked me from that nightmare. This safe house in San Diego feels like a dream in comparison.

"Roja!" he snaps, jerking me from my thoughts.

I nod rapidly and slide my palms higher along his thighs. Anything to coax him out of this tense mood he's in. "I'm yours."

His features relax, and I feel proud that I've pleased him. Maybe he'll fix me a giant sandwich with extra turkey and—

"He must not find out about…" he trails off and scratches his jaw as if to search for the correct word. "He must not find out about how you and I came to be a couple."

I may not be drugged up on heroin like my mother, but Esteban is definitely running through my veins. I don't understand how he burrowed his way under my skin. Months ago, I hated him. Now, my skin tingles at the mention of the word couple.

Deep down inside, a part of me screams. It's a silent scream, but I feel it in my bones.

He stole you. He raped you. He killed your mother. Fuck Esteban.

But since he's bubbling in my veins like the hot liquid drug that makes strong people weak, thoughts of him silence the part of me that screams in protest.

Esteban saved you from the metal box.

Esteban saved you from the stench of your mother's rotting corpse.

Esteban brought you to this home to feed and care for you.

"I love when you look at me that way, Roja," he murmurs, lust thick in his voice. "I want to see those adoring eyes on me while you worship my cock."

A smile touches my lips as my fingers skate along the hard outline of his erection in his slacks to his belt. He usually feeds me after sex, but especially if I blow him. Eager to not only please him but also to eat, I yank at the leather and work frantically to free his dick. I'm overwhelmed with the need to please him. The past few days have been heaven with him trapping me beneath him while he fucks me wildly. After all those months in the metal box, this life with him is manageable. I'm safe and cared for under his watch. Today, though, he's regarded me differently, and I hate it. I want the look of desire back in his eyes. The pure, unfiltered look of possession. And I want a damn sandwich.

His cock is hot in my hand the second I grip my fingers around it. My mouth waters to lick his tip and show him how good I can be for him. He lets out a slight hiss of air when my thumb runs along the side of his shaft, which is all I need to dive in. I slide my parted lips over the head of his length and let my tongue taste the underside of him. A grunt rumbles from him as he takes handfuls of my hair on each side of my head. His grip isn't harsh, like it sometimes can be. It's just firm enough to guide me the way he likes.

I work him up and down with my fist while dancing circles with my tongue. His girth is wide enough to make my jaw ache, but not bad enough that I can't push him deep into my throat. The moment I relax my muscles and swallow him, he lets out a string of curse words in Spanish. I smile against his cock but don't slow my movements. I'm about to pop off of him for a moment to catch my breath, but his grip on my hair stops me. His hips thrust up as he shoves my face against him. His sudden deep intrusion causes me to gag. Drool runs out of my mouth and along his cock while I wriggle to get away.

"That's it," he hisses. "Take every inch."

Tears from not being able to breathe stream down my cheeks. I dig my fingernails into his thighs to let him know I can't take any more. This only seems to turn him on more because with a long grunt and an extra brutal thrust of his hips, he comes down the back of my throat.

I gag and gag but thankfully don't throw up—not that there's anything in my belly to expel, anyway. Finally, when

I feel as though I might black out, he releases me. I jerk off his cock and gasp for air. Snot runs from my nose and down over my lips.

His face is impassive as he sets to putting his cock back inside his boxers and slacks. I stare at his features while they're distracted.

He will always be like this. Remember what he did to your best friend?

I silence my inner screamer with a flash of inner rage. My best friend abandoned me. Married into the family I was supposed to marry into, dragging grown men on their knees behind her in her wake. Oscar had been drawn to her. Duvan had fallen for her. And Esteban had fucked her.

Thoughts go to my father...

Daddy was obsessed with her and now he's gone.

While Brie was off living the good life, I'd been stolen by the man who hurt her. I was starved and beaten and fucked right out of my sanity. I was forced to listen to my mother die in a metal cage. All because Brie made smart men stupid. All because Brie was too selfish to come for me.

If the situation were reversed, I would have gone for her.

Tears don't fall, though. Instead, anger bubbles in my chest. This is my world now. Esteban may not be perfect, but at least he wants me. Unlike Oscar. Unlike Brie. Unlike anyone else.

"You're to do exactly as I say," Esteban growls as he tugs me into his lap.

My eyes find his and I straddle his muscular thighs. I can't help but touch him with greedy fingers. I'm sure I look a mess with my drool and snot and watery eyes, but he looks at me as though I'm perfect.

"Of course," I tell him with a smile. "Can you feed me now?"

He smirks before pulling me against him. "Oh, Roja," he says with a chuckle. "I just fed you." His fingertips stroke me until I'm dozing off. I inhale his scent and it reminds me of the first time I smelled him up close. It helps the pain in my belly disappear.

"Ozzy?" I question as I peek inside another door. My parents and I just arrived at the Rojas's for the summer. I'm dying to find him and hope he notices I'm wearing makeup. Daddy made me wait until I turned fourteen to start wearing it. Well, I'm fourteen now, so Oscar will have to notice me.

I adjust my push-up bra and wander along the hallway until I get a whiff of weed. My nose scrunches at the smell, but I follow it in hopes it'll lead to Ozzy. When I push through the door, I enter a darkened room. Dark curtains cover the window, and the only light comes from a black light on the wall.

"Oscar?"

A female giggles, and I jerk my head over to see a woman straddling Duvan's lap. She's blowing smoke into his mouth. My gaze lingers on them. Duvan is several years older than Ozzy and I. Where my best friend is lanky and boyish, Duvan is all man. He's in college now and has muscles.

I'm still staring at them when Duvan seems to notice me. "Vienna. Did you lose your way from your mommy?"

The dark-haired woman in his lap jerks her head to glare at me and then laughs upon seeing me. Her boobs are giant and bounce with her giggles. I suddenly feel like a kid in comparison. I mean…I am only fourteen but most days I feel grown up. Not today, though. Today I'm staring at her chest, wishing for humongous breasts like hers.

"I was looking for Oscar," I tell him, dragging my gaze from the woman's chest.

Duvan smirks and accepts more smoke from the woman who's no longer interested in me. His hands lazily roam her butt while I stare in wonder. Maybe one day, Oscar will touch me like that. I'll have boobs, and he'll want to squeeze them with his hands.

"I should go," I murmur and start to back out.

"You should stay." The deep voice behind me causes me to jump.

Esteban.

He's the scary brother.

When I turn around, he's staring at me like I'm a little mouse with its leg caught in a trap. Like he's a big cat with sharp teeth and he wants to shred my flesh straight from my body. I shiver but attempt to calm myself. Esteban won't do anything to me—not with Daddy downstairs. My dad would kill him.

"Sit, Roja," Esteban commands, his eyes unnaturally white and evil looking in the black light. "Hang out with the adults for awhile."

When I don't move, he grabs my elbow and ushers me into Duvan's room and over to the sofa. I'm forced to sit. Esteban sits down beside me and stretches out his long legs. He's a giant compared to Ozzy. When I look at Esteban, I see someone who's no longer the young teen from my youth. He's this grown man—a man who's done terrible things, based on what Oscar has told me. I don't like him one bit.

"You smoke?" he questions as he leans across me to access the side table.

His masculine scent envelops me, and I shiver.

"I haven't tried it, no."

Duvan is too busy playing with his girlfriend to notice that his brother is attempting to get me high. My daddy will be so angry if he finds out I've been up here with these men.

"Nice bra," Esteban says with a wolfish grin.

I snap my gaze down and gape in horror. My tight light-orange T-shirt is practically transparent in the weird lighting. The white push up bra underneath glows!

"Oh my God," I shriek and cross my arms over my chest.

He laughs at me as he lights a joint. I watch the way his stubbly cheeks suck in as he inhales. The way his full lips part and the smoke billows from his mouth. Then, he smirks and hands it to me.

"Your turn."

When I don't reach for it, he shrugs. "Didn't take you for a pussy, niñita. Guess I was wrong."

Fire flashes inside me, and I snap the joint out of his hand. I bring it to my lips and attempt to mimic his actions. As soon as the strange smoke fills my lungs, I start coughing. Esteban's booming laughter upsets me as I choke. When I can finally breathe normally again, I glare at him.

"Rude."

He shrugs and slings an arm over my shoulders, hugging me to him. "Tell me something I don't know."

I relax against his hold and attempt to remain calm. I've been following these boys around alongside Oscar for as long as I can remember. The fact that they're finally letting me hang *out with them makes me happy—even if they are having fun at my expense.*

"I used to think this house was a castle," I tell him. My body is starting to feel loose. Free even. "Your dad is the beast of the castle." I start to giggle, imaging Mr. Rojas big and furry like Beast from my favorite childhood movie.

Esteban chuckles as he takes another hit of the joint. His fingers are dragging up and down along my arm, making me feel tingly. "What am I then, princess?"

Moans start coming from the other side of the room, and I drift my gaze over to where Duvan has his hand under the woman's skirt. She rocks against him as if she's enjoying it. It makes me wonder exactly what he's doing under there.

I look up at Esteban. His eyes have turned nearly black and he looks completely chill. Nice even. I start to giggle again, which makes him grin. "You're the snake in the garden."

"Like from the Bible?" He smirks, and it reminds me of Oscar.

Where is that boy, anyway?

"Yep. And I'm not a princess, I'm the—"

"Angel?"

I snort and shake my head. "No, the queen."

His brows scrunch together. "Queen, huh?"

"Queen of everything."

"Is that right, Roja?"

"And I'm going to rule the world one day."

He inspects me with a narrowed gaze and passes me the joint. This time, I don't choke. It sucks that Oscar isn't around. It'd be even more fun with him here.

"I'm sleepy."

"Sleep then."

I drag my eyelids open but they feel heavy. I'm not sure why I'm so out of it. My thoughts linger in the past. I can almost smell the weed. Curling against Esteban, I close my eyes again. That day when I'd smoked pot with him, I'd woken up on the couch alone. When I sat up to try and figure out where I was, I realized that although I was fully dressed, my bra was gone.

"You took my bra off that day while I slept, didn't you?" I question softly.

He chuckles, and it reminds me so much of that day. "I wanted it. And I take what I want."

II | Oscar

I STARE AT MY BROTHER FROM ACROSS THE TABLE AT THE safe house and truly inspect him. It's been months since I last saw him. When he all but vanished after fucking up one of my best friends. My own brother fucked and drugged his brother's wife. Duvan had wanted to kill him but never got the chance.

An ache forms in my chest for the loss of my brother. And that ache only grows when I think about my father on his knees in the shipping container, desperately trying to hold the wounds in his stomach closed. I watched my father die that day. Watched him bleed out and collapse to the floor. It was as though Brie held his fate in her hands because she asked Diego to kill him. To my surprise, the motherfucker obeyed her. That's something I'll never be able to forgive her for. Colluding with a Rojas enemy is unforgivable.

I close my eyes for a brief moment but that only makes the memory more vivid. Quickly, I stare back at the man who is the only family I have left. My brother's dark eyes are narrowed and his jaw is clenched. The silvery scar that runs down the side of his face glistens under the light of the dining room table. I'd been eleven years old the day he got it. I watched my badass brother get his ass kicked by someone somehow scarier than him. All over a girl.

He reaches up and scratches at the dark hair that speckles his jaw as he scrutinizes me with a guarded expression. His hair once used to be closely shaved to his head, but it's long since grown out. Esteban looks more like Duvan and I when he has the unruliness about him. More passionate than calculating.

"Where is she?" My tone is calm even though my hands clench into fists.

"I've been taking care of her. She's sleeping right now."

The anxiety that's been swarming in my stomach like a storm of pissed-off bees lessens. "You didn't hurt her? Where's she been since her dad was killed? Where's her mother?"

He crosses his arms over his chest and leans back. Esteban is always dressed nicely. Duvan took a page from his book and dressed the same. Our father instilled that in us. *Dress like kings because you are all my little princes.* Now that Papá is gone, I dress how I want. Compared to my older brother, I'm nothing but a boy dressed sloppily in jeans and a T-shirt.

"Vee is not hurt," he tells me, his voice carrying a slight edge to it. "Her mother is off somewhere being the whore she always was. I've helped Vee manage the properties by paying the bills for her."

I let out a sigh of relief. "Can you wake her? I miss her."

Vee has been one of my closest friends since the day

she showed up in our kitchen, covered in blood at the age of five. I remember thinking she was sort of scary, but when she smiled all fear evaporated. We'd been connected at the hip ever since. For the longest time, we'd even thought our fathers would arrange for us to marry. It seemed logical, but we both knew our hearts weren't in it. A marriage between the Berkleys and the Rojas' would have been on paper only. At least for our parents, anyway. But she was my best friend, and I'd always imagined I'd fall deeply in love with her the way she seemed to love me. *One day.*

"Let her sleep," Esteban says and pushes a bottle of tequila my way. "Tonight, we drink. I've missed you, hermanito."

I take a swig from the bottle and enjoy the way it burns my throat. It seems to sharpen my senses, something I am thankful for. Ever since Papá was brutally murdered by Diego Gomez, my mind has been muddled with confusion, heartache, and an all-consuming thirst for vengeance. The only thing that takes the edge off are the pills I take from time to time—something has to calm me the fuck down. Now that I'm here with Esteban, though, we can begin to formulate a plan and deal with this shit, so I don't have to obsess over it all the damn time.

"I want to kill him," I tell him in a blunt tone and swallow down more of the fiery tequila.

Esteban snags the bottle from me and takes a swallow. "Who are we killing?"

I growl and slam my fist on the table. "Diego!"

He narrows his gaze at me. "Diego is the most powerful man in Colombia right now. You think you're going to stomp right in there and kill him without any sort of resistance?"

My chest deflates as his words sink in. Anger consumes

me but I have no outlet for it. "So we make a plan."

"We have no men," Esteban reminds me. "It will take some time to talk to Papá's and Duvan's men so that we can begin to gather our army. These things don't happen overnight, Oz."

I run my fingers through my wild hair. It now hangs in my eyes, but I can't be bothered to cut it. I'm sure to my put-together brother, I look like a bratty kid. That's how he's always seen me. But inside…inside I am raging like a beast. Duvan always favored our mother. And I thought perhaps I was like her too. At one time, maybe I was. Now, though, I am different. Anger throbs within me, like some uncaged beast waiting to be set free. Sometimes, when I look in the mirror, I don't see myself. I see the cold eyes of my father.

"He took our home."

Esteban is mid swallow when his eyes meet mine. "W-What?"

"After Diego killed Papá, he went back to Colombia and he took our childhood home," I hiss. "The same home Mami died in. He just moved the fuck in there like he's the goddamned king of our castle."

Esteban's eyes blaze with rage. He's normally calm and collected, but I know I struck a nerve. When our mother died, I think all the humanity in Esteban died with her. He'd taken it the hardest. It was at that point, I didn't know my brother anymore. All memories of us playing in the woods by our house and Esteban saving me from drowning in a nearby river when I was a toddler were wiped clean.

"We have to get it back," he growls and chugs more of the tequila before passing it back to me.

"We will."

His black eyebrows pinch together, and I can see the wheels turning in his head. My brother is smart. Together we'll devise a plan.

Over the next two hours, we become more and more drunk. Our plans to take over the world are interrupted when a flash of red darts into the kitchen. Esteban is leaned back in his chair with his feet on the table, looking relaxed as fuck.

But as soon as she comes into view, we both sober up fairly quickly.

"Ozzy?"

Vee's bright green eyes are wide and innocent looking. Her pink lips are parted in surprise at seeing me. Her trademark wild red mane is in messy tangles all over her head as if she hasn't brushed it in quite some time. Of course she's cute as ever—always has been—but what has my attention are her tits.

"Why are you naked?" I choke out, my dick hardening in my jeans. Once, at her apartment, she'd begged through her tears for me to take her virginity. Back then, I was a different man. I had morals and valued our friendship. Sure, I couldn't help but kiss her but I did refrain from popping her cherry. But now? Fuck…I'd hit that for damn sure.

Esteban growls and reaches for her. Her eyes tear away from mine to find his. The small moment of clarity seems to dissipate as she gets a glassy-eyed look. A small smile forms on her pouty lips. She all but runs to him. I gape in confusion as she sits in his lap and curls against him.

What the fuck is happening?

"Vee?" I snap, and ask again, through gritted teeth, "Why are you naked?"

Esteban strokes her messy hair and levels me with a hard gaze. "We're together, and she wasn't expecting company."

My gaze is fixated on her perfectly rounded tits. I have no words. I have no idea what the hell is going on. This is far from what I expected to find here. If she's "together" with Esteban, there's no doubt in my mind they're fucking. The thought that she isn't a virgin anymore saddens me. I guess I always thought she'd be there when I was ready.

"Can you put some clothes on?" I hiss through clenched teeth. There's no way I can carry on this conversation with her succulent tits on full display. She looks up at Esteban in question. As if she needs permission from him to dress. A flash of fire blazes inside me. This isn't the Vee I know. The Vee I know isn't controlled by anyone.

"Take my shirt," he tells her and strokes her cheek.

She leans in to his touch and smiles. It's creepy as fuck.

"Thank you," she murmurs as she starts delicately plucking through his buttons. Once she unfastens them all, he slips out of his dress shirt and helps her into it. He fastens one button in front of her tits before pulling her against his chest.

"How long you two been together?" I question, my voice coming out with a slight bite.

Vee stiffens for a brief moment but won't meet my gaze. "Months now, right Esteban?"

He continues to pet her and nods. "Yep. Might even be love." His gaze darts to mine and he smirks. The look says, *I won the fucking prize*. It makes my blood boil. Vee is *my* age. She was *my* friend growing up. She was *mine*.

Was.

She looks up at him in confusion. "Love?"

18

Esteban shrugs and runs his thumb across her bottom lip. "Could be. You hungry, Roja?"

Vee has pretty smiles. But the one she's giving him right now is unlike any other I've seen before. Brilliant like a thousand rays of sunlight.

"Please," she begs. "I'm so hungry."

He pushes her off his lap and gives her ass a little pinch. "Go take a quick shower, and I'll have it ready for you."

She lets out a squeal before throwing her arms around his neck. "Thank you!" Her lips find his and they kiss as if they're in a goddamned porno. It fucking nauseates me.

When she's gone, he rises and begins making a sandwich. He pours her a giant glass of milk. Then, he reaches into his pocket, retrieves a pill, crushes it with a knife, and drops the dust crumbles into the milk.

I scowl. "What the fuck did you just put in her drink?"

His eyes pierce mine. "She likes it. Mind your own fucking business."

Those words cut through me, and I'm transported to the past.

"Mind your own fucking business," Esteban growls.

I ignore the sounds of Duvan banging Luz in the corner. Her little sister and I go to school together. Both Luz and Ana are skanks. I don't know why Duvan sleeps with her. Everyone has slept with Luz and Ana. I know for a fact Esteban has been with Luz, too. And just yesterday, Ana sucked my dick between classes.

"Why do you have her bra?" I demand through clenched teeth. I may only be halfway through fourteen years of age, but I would try to kick his ass if I had to. Of course Esteban would pummel me, but I bet I'd get a hit or two in on him.

"She gave it to me," he says simply and brings one of the white padded cups to his nose to inhale. "So sweet."

I glare at him and then dart my gaze down to Vee. Her shirt is still on, but now I can see her small nipples through the fabric. She's sleeping peacefully. Did she really give it to him?

"Leave her alone," I mutter in defeat. "She deserves some-one better than you fucking with her."

He smirks. "Like you? Have you stolen her V-card yet, Oz?"

"No," I snap.

"Why not? You've racked up quite the collection of V-cards lately, haven't you? Duvan tells me you've fucked your way through most of the girls at your school."

Irritation bubbles through me. "Vee's my friend. It's not like that."

"Ahhh," he says with a malicious grin. "So I'm free to take it."

"Fuck you!"

I hear a zipper behind me, and then Duvan saunters up next to me wearing nothing but a pair of jeans and stinking like sex. He slings an arm over my shoulder. I can tell he's high as fuck.

"Why are you two assholes fighting in my room?" Duvan questions, a lazy smile on his face.

I ignore him and squat down in front of the sofa. Vee looks so innocent with her head in Esteban's lap as she sleeps. Doesn't she know my brother is evil? I slide my arms beneath her to lift her up, but Esteban's giant hand pushes down on her breast through her shirt to keep me from lifting her.

"She stays," he taunts, a challenge gleaming in his eyes.

"Take your hand off of her before I break it," I snarl and meet his glare. "She goes with me."

Both him and Duvan start laughing at my valiant effort to protect my friend. I'm able to snag her and escape without any more crap from the two assholes. Once she's settled in my dark room under the blankets, I crawl in behind her to spoon her.

She's my best friend, and I'll be damned if I let them fuck with her.

"I missed you, Ozzy," she murmurs, half asleep.

"Missed you too, Vee. Now sleep this shit off so your dad doesn't kill us."

She squirms a little, which makes my cock harden against her ass. I'll have to go visit Ana later to get laid or I'll end up doing something stupid like fucking my best friend. The image of her naked and beneath me only makes my cock harder, so I try to envision other things that don't turn me on. Like Esteban, the fucker. But then my active imagination goes to him with Vee underneath him. His teeth on her tiny tits, marking her up like some kind of savage beast. My erection is gone but now I'm just raging with fury. With Vee turning into a woman, she'll start to be a problem when she visits. Esteban likes to conquer and Duvan likes to fuck. Between the two of them, one of them will corrupt her if I don't protect her.

"I'll keep you safe," I assure her in the faintest of whispers.

I'm snapped from my inner thoughts when a fresh-faced Vee

bounces into the kitchen. Her eyes glitter with excitement, which makes my chest ache. At one time, she wanted me. Not him. Me. And now, one of the few people I have left in this world doesn't want me anymore.

"I'm so hungry," she tells Esteban as she eyeballs the sandwich he's set out for her on the table.

"I know. Sit." He motions for the chair that he's dragged right beside him. "Eat."

Her red hair looks darker now that it's wet. It hasn't been combed through and she isn't wearing any makeup whatsoever. It makes her seem younger, like that night I rescued her from Esteban's predator ass when she was just fourteen.

I guess it's too late to rescue her now. She's clearly head over fucking heels for him. Every look she flashes him is filled with adoration and love. I'm completely ignored. As she starts to eat, Esteban leans forward to watch her. She devours the sandwich in record speed. Then, she chugs the milk. It isn't until she finishes that I remember him putting something in it.

Fuck.

I'm the worst goddamned friend ever.

"Can I have more?" she pleads with him, sadness pulling on her cute features. "Please."

He pats her while he shakes his head. "No. Not right now. I don't want you to get sick."

She frowns but obeys. "Okay."

"Let's go outside on the porch and talk," Esteban says as he stands. She takes his hand as if it's normal and lets him guide her outside. I stare after them. The shirt he made her wear swallows her, but it's white and completely see-through. It's like she's fucked in the head or something.

I snag the tequila bottle and make my way outside. It's dark and the ocean is fairly volatile as a storm starts to roll in. The wind is brusque and way too cold for her to be out here with no clothes on. Esteban is just wearing his wife beater, so I'm sure he's cold too. But neither of them seem bothered as they sit down in the wicker love seat. I sit across from them in a single chair.

Esteban and I discuss Diego Gomez. We each state what we know of his territory and inner workings. And as the night progresses, the liquor begins to numb me to my core. Esteban becomes more handsy, while Vee seems to squirm with need. Whatever he gave her appears to be working because she is practically humping his leg.

We've all gone quiet. The two of them are wrapped up in each other while I stare like some perverted voyeur. I guess I don't get how she's suddenly so into my brother. Everyone always knew Vee wanted me. I knew this. Vee knew this. Our friends and family. But I cared for her as a friend, which always had me keeping my dick in my pants. There were so many times when I could have fucked her, and she would have let me. I didn't, though.

And now, apparently, the time has passed.

My best friend has moved on to my fucking brother instead.

Vee wasn't ever supposed to be his.

I'm still lost in thought when I hear the pop of a button and then see a flash of white as the shirt falls to the floor. Her back is to me and she's straddling my brother's lap. I've seen both my brothers fucking before. Plenty of times. But seeing my best friend all but beg for my brother's cock definitely pisses me off. What pisses me off more is that the curve of

23

her ass has my cock harder than fucking stone.

Vee wasn't ever supposed to be his.

My gaze stays on her ass as she rubs herself against him through his slacks. Her fingers are locked in his hair and she keeps begging.

"Please, Esteban."

Her breathy tone is too much. I've never craved Vee sexually. Sure, I'd thought about boning her a time or two, because I was a horny little shit, but never once did I just crave her. Yet now, I can't stop thinking about her full tits and round ass. About the fact that my brother will soon be inside her.

I rub at my cock through my jeans, seeking relief. When I lift my gaze, I see that my brother caught the movement. He smirks, like all those times he'd fucked a woman in front of me before. A smirk that says, *it's okay, you can watch and maybe learn a thing or two.*

My jaw clenches when I hear the buckle of his belt jangle. Soon, he's got his pants pushed down his thighs. Then, I hear the tear of a condom packet. He's about to fuck her right in front of me. I should just get up and let them do their shit. I don't want to fucking see this.

But I don't move.

I do want to see.

"Oz is turned on, Roja," he growls. "Let my baby brother see what's mine." He grabs her hips and twists her so that she's facing me. My gaze falls to her large tits, which bounce with her movement, and then roam over her flat stomach to the thin tuft of red hair between her thighs. I can see my brother's dick sliding in and out of her. Her juices soaking his cock. I let out a groan as my eyes travel back up her creamy curves to her face.

"Mmm," she murmurs as she rubs at her nipples.

My brother grips her hair and yanks her back. Her tits stick out even farther. I'm aching to fist my cock right now. Vee looks so fucking hot, and I'm a damn idiot for not ever hitting that before. Her full lips are swollen and parted as she moans. Those green eyes—eyes that always light up with the fire typical of redheads—have been dulled. She's high as fuck on whatever he gave her.

"Whom do you belong to?" Esteban murmurs as he thrusts his hips up.

She shudders. "You."

Vee wasn't ever supposed to be his.

My cock is seriously straining in my jeans now. I can't fucking deal with how painful it is so I unzip my jeans and free it. When I start stroking myself, I pretend that it's me she's riding. I bet her pussy is so goddamned tight.

"Ahh," Esteban taunts. "Baby brother can't control himself around you."

I don't look at him but instead meet her gaze. The adoration she used to look at me with is vacant from her eyes. Instead, all I find there is desperation. Desperation to reach that high she's chasing.

Vee wasn't ever supposed to be his.

Her eyes lock on my cock and she bites her lip. It's when she lets out a moan as an orgasm overtakes her that I lose it. Hot semen shoots up my chest, wetting my T-shirt. My cock throbs as I drain the rest of my release. The moment I come down from my climax, reality sets in.

I just got off watching my rapist brother fuck my high-off-her-ass best friend.

I'm a fucking asshole.

III | Vee

THE ROOM SPINS AROUND ME AS ESTEBAN CARRIES ME inside. Everything is so foggy lately. Like I'm in a dream. And all I want to do is eat and fuck. As if I'm some animal.

"I'm hungry," I whine when Esteban lays me on the mattress.

"Tomorrow," he tells me and stumbles into the bathroom. When he emerges some time later, he's clean from a shower but still looks drunk. He falls into the bed face first.

Even through my haze, I realize this is the first time he's dropped his guard since he's had me here at this San Diego safe house. My brain is garbled and confused. A part of me feels like this is important. That I should do something about it. But a bigger part of me wonders if he'll notice if I sneak out to make a sandwich. My stomach growls as if to answer me.

Eventually, after what feels like hours, I decide to sneak out. The only goal in my head is food. I stumble through the darkness, now that all of the lights have been shut off, in a journey to the kitchen. I'm careful as I tiptoe into the kitchen. I'll just sneak a banana or something and slip back into bed. Esteban will never know. As quietly as I can, I open the cupboards on a hunt for something quick and edible. I find the jar of peanut butter, which makes my stomach growl again. Quickly, I twist off the top and stick my finger inside to scoop out some. It tastes so good that I let out an embarrassing moan. I'm scooping out another heap with my fingers when I sense someone else's presence.

Jerking my head toward the doorway, I'm shocked to see Ozzy standing there in nothing but his boxers. His hair is messy like he's been sleeping. Now that I'm getting some food in my belly, I'm able to wade through some of the fog.

"I was hungry," I murmur as I suck on my finger.

His eyes darken and he prowls forward. Old familiar feelings stir in my belly. So many times I imagined scenes where he'd find me naked and then claim me. Lust swims in his gaze. Desire for me.

Esteban would kill him for looking at me like that.

"He doesn't let you wear clothes?" he questions, his voice husky as he steps closer.

I shake my head. "No."

He sways on his feet and I remember how much tequila he drank earlier. When he grips my wrist, I let out a whimper. I watch with sadness as he draws my peanut-butter-covered fingers to his mouth. My stomach continues to growl, and yet, here he is sucking the precious food off my hand.

"You're a natural seductress," he tells me as he licks his lips. Then, his mouth sucks on two of my fingers at a time. My nipples harden and I hate that my body responds to him.

Esteban made it very clear that my feelings for Oscar were over.

"I just want to eat," I tell him.

He pushes my hand between my thighs and smears the creamy goodness still left on my fingers along the lips of my pussy. "So do I."

I start to argue but then he's on his knees. His mouth is on me, sucking off the peanut butter with vigor. I nearly drop the vat of peanut butter on his head. Stars glitter in my vision. My mind is still foggy, but I feel a niggling sensation creeping over me. Telling me this is wrong. That this will get me in a lot of trouble.

What if Esteban makes me go back to the metal box?

What if I starve again?

A tear snakes its way down my cheek, and I desperately shovel more peanut butter into my mouth. His tongue is on my clit, lapping at me as he licks away the food he smeared there. Small jolts of pleasure prickle through me here and there, but I mostly wish he would stop before everything blows up in our faces. I let out a groan when he urges my leg over his shoulder. His mouth cleans every single smudge of peanut butter off my pussy.

"You're so hot," he breathes against me.

I frown as I suck more peanut butter off my fingers. "Please stop."

He presses a kiss to my clit before standing. His lips are quirked up into the mischievous smile I remember so well. It makes my heart squeeze from the memory of how I used to feel about him.

"Did you come?" he questions as he steals my jar from me.

I growl. "Give it back."

"There she is. Guess the mollies or whatever the fuck he gave to you are fading. The bitch is waking up," he says with relief.

My eyes are fixated on the jar of peanut butter. I can't believe he stole it from me. I'm so damn hungry. Anger surges through me, and I attempt to take it back, but he holds it high over his head.

"While my tongue was between your legs, I came up with a plan. Tomorrow, we're going to Colombia."

I freeze and stare at him. "I'm staying with Esteban."

He gives me back my peanut butter and then sets to wetting a cloth. I'm too focused on my only source of food to even notice that he cleans me up between my legs.

"Vee," he tells me with a smile. "I have a plan to take back what belongs to our families. You'll be a Rojas one day, so this should be important to you."

A Rojas?

For so many years I wanted that…but with Oscar.

Now, I try to imagine being married to his brother.

My fantasies are jumbled and messy. Right now I don't think I like them either way. A thundering in my head starts to form again as I try to work out my future.

I don't want to believe it but I know, deep down, Esteban is drugging me and probably has been for some time.

That has to be why I'm so out of it. So animalistic.

The only thing that explains the headaches and confusion.

"Go to sleep. Tomorrow, we're going to war. And you, Vee," he says with a smile as he strokes my cheek, "are going to help us."

"What is this place?" I question as I peer out a window that faces a pond. The dress that sticks to my body feels heavy and strange after months of not wearing anything. When I don't get a response, I turn to regard Esteban.

His arms are crossed over his chest while he glares at me as if the dress disgusts him as well. But we traveled to Colombia, and I couldn't exactly do it naked. I shiver under his gaze.

"Where are we?" I ask again, my voice softer this time. Now that the fog no longer confuses me and the headaches aren't crushing me, I've had a lot of time to think. I've had a lot of time to remember.

He took me and my mother. Seeing the gun pressed against my mother's temple was all the incentive I needed to willingly follow Esteban. Had I known I was subjecting myself to dark isolation for months in a metal box, I'd have run for the hills. Had I known he'd force his cock into me while I screamed in pain, I'd have put up a bigger fight. Had I known he'd make me watch my mother become addicted to heroin only to have to watch her die later, I'd have tried to kill him.

But I didn't know. Deep down, I trusted him not to hurt me. I thought we had history. I'd assumed that because our fathers had been business partners and I visited the Rojas's every summer, that Esteban would have a soft spot for me.

And yet he hurt me.

So many times.

He was the deliverer of pain, but then he'd follow it up

with pleasure. All those nights in that dark box, he'd turned me into some sexually hungry animal that fed off of him. Now that my mind has cleared, I know he drugged me then too. I'd been too out of my head to understand it for what it was.

He. Drugged. Me.

Just like my mother.

Just like Brie.

My heart squeezes at the thought of my adopted sister and best friend, other than Oscar. When Daddy told me he was adopting her, I'd been elated. I thought he wanted me to have a friend being that I was home schooled and lonely. Later, I learned he adopted her to take my place as the betrothed to the Rojas family. At the time, I was embarrassed but having her in my life has outweighed all of that.

If she were here, my feisty friend would tell me what to do. She'd tell me to get away from Esteban—that he's a monster. I bet she would even help me, too.

I swallow down the emotion in my throat. The last thing I need is for these two men to see me weak. I'll have to figure out what to do on my own.

I'm a Berkley.

A badass bitch.

I just need to be a calculating bitch.

It takes everything inside of me to remain calm and not fly off the handle. I need to be smart. Going off on Esteban for everything he's done seems like a dangerous move. And I still can't argue the way he makes me feel when it's just the two of us. That's the most frustrating part of it all. Despite my eagerness to make him pay, I still can't deny the way my pussy seems to flare to life around him. He truly did train my body. But he'll never own my mind as long as I have anything to say about it.

"Papá's safe house," Ozzy answers as he strolls into the room. My nostrils flare when I see him. Of course he looks sexy as ever in his playboy Ozzy way, but it doesn't excite me like it used to. Instead, irritation bubbles up inside me.

"So what's the plan?" I question as I let my gaze dart back and forth between the two men who each have their own special grip on my heart.

"It's better if you don't know the plan," Oscar says plainly.

I scowl at him and give Esteban a pleading look that sometimes works on him when he's being soft. His gaze loses some of its hardness as he holds a hand out to me. My gut instinct tells me to demand they tell me what's going on. To stomp my feet and scream at them both until I get my way. But the brain that had been locked away while Esteban kept me has begun to work full throttle again. And because of that, I go willingly to Esteban.

His arm snakes around my waist and he pulls me possessively against him. "I don't like the plan."

"Don't tell her," Ozzy warns.

The fire explodes inside of me, and I twist to glare at him. "Tell me the damn plan, asshole!"

Hurt flashes in his eyes, but I don't care. Oscar has given me the puppy dog eyes one too many times, and right now, I'm immune. Who knows? Maybe they'll never work on me again.

"Roja," Esteban murmurs as his lips find my neck. "The plan is fucking stupid."

"So what's plan B then?" I question as my eyes flutter closed. When he's touching me, I lose all sense of reality. That smart little brain shuts off and lets my pussy call the shots.

"There is no plan B. It's plan V," Oscar grunts. "You're the plan."

I tug away to unlatch myself from Esteban's dizzying kisses on my throat. "Care to explain?"

Esteban twists me in his arms so that we're facing each other. His hand slides to my throat and he holds me gently. "Women are his weakness. We'll use you to infiltrate his operation from the inside out. He has too many men to just attack. You'll kill him and then, by the time his men are in chaos over what to do after that happens, we'll have amassed our own men to take over." He growls and anger gleams in his dark eyes. "He stole our childhood home. We want it back."

I blink at him in confusion. "You want to send me straight to him? To flirt with him until his back is turned, and then what? Stab him in the back? I've never killed anyone before!" My chest heaves as I freak out. Are these two knuckleheads insane? They want me to invade this guy's life and kill him just because they want their stupid house back? This is the worst idea ever.

"Not flirt," Esteban snaps. "Fuck."

White heat colors my vision as fury seeps its way into my bones. Anger is a safer emotion than the terror that barely hides behind it. "What?" My voice is shrill. "But I thought I was yours!"

The monster that sometimes presents itself in his eyes rages forward. "You. *Are*. Mine. And the moment we have our shit back, I'm going to marry you and put fucking babies inside of you. But first," he snarls, his grip on my throat tightening. "First we fight. First we take."

My hands fist at my sides, but I refuse to lose control

right now. I'm not one hundred percent myself so I need to chill the hell out before I make the wrong move. If Daddy ever taught me anything, it was to always know my enemy. It was to outsmart them all. He was so smart and successful. I can do this.

"He'll be suspicious. Won't he figure out who my father is? Won't he know I'm connected to you guys?" I hiss out my questions until Esteban releases my throat. I rub at my flesh and pin him with a fiery glare. "What if I don't *want* to have sex with him? What if he hurts me?" My voice cracks. "I'm scared." I will not cry. I will not whine. But a part of me is upset and furious. This thing with Esteban is wrong and fucked up, but it's the only evil I know right now. He even said babies and marriage. So why do I once again just feel like a pawn in their game? A little girl in a room full of big bad wolves.

Oscar lets out a snide laugh. "You're pretty good at shaking your tits when you want something. So shake your tits for Diego and kill him. Then you get what you so desperately want." He motions for Esteban, but I don't miss the flicker of jealousy in his eyes. At one time, I wanted to see that look so badly. Today it's infuriating me.

"You want to be a Rojas? Well, then there are just certain things you must do," Esteban snaps with a shrug. "This is one of them."

I'm stung by his words. "But—"

His fingers crush into my jaw as he draws me closer. "No buts. You do this and we move on. You don't fuck any other men ever again."

Rage is blooming up inside of me. My head is clear—so fucking crystal clear—and I can see the big picture. How could I let myself get caught up in this man? He's been toying with me since I was a child.

Emotion chokes me, but I refuse to cry. I wish Brie were here. The thought once again hits me like a sucker punch to my gut. She was a victim. *I* am a victim. Pain slices through my chest as realization sets in. She was never the villain.

The villain is right in front of me.

He presses a soft kiss to my lips, and I fight the urge to bite him.

"So tonight," Oscar says with a growl, "we implement part one of the plan. Then, we deliver you right to his den."

Terror fights its way up inside of me. What if this Diego is like their father? Camilo always scared me half to death. I'm headed for some crazy old man's house to let him fuck me so I can kill him in his sleep. Fucking wonderful.

"But—" I start, but Esteban crams something into my mouth.

An acrid taste makes me gag, but he pushes the pill toward the back of my throat until I'm forced to swallow.

"This should make you more compliant," Esteban says before he shoves me away from him.

I blink after him in confusion as he storms away, leaving me with Oscar. Jerking my head over my shoulder, I see him prowling forward. I'm about to lay into him when he rears his fist back and socks me in the eye.

I gape at him in horror and implore him with my stare as my trembling fingers touch my face that now screams in pain. Our eyes meet for a brief moment, and I search his gaze for guilt or sorrow or anything to indicate what just happened was an accident.

He clenches his jaw and his dark eyes are wild but regret

swims just beneath the surface of his glare. I'm about to tearfully throw myself into his arms when he pulls his fist back again. The pain this time, as my best friend cracks me in the face, is overwhelming.

Make that my *ex* best friend.

The innocent boy I once knew has been slaughtered by this animal.

I crumple to the floor like a sack of potatoes and my world immediately fades to black.

I want to open my eyes but they feel too heavy. My mind is a cloud of darkness as I try and make sense of my surroundings. I can hear water running.

God, my face hurts. I groan and try to reach out for something to ground me. Whatever I'm touching is soft.

A bed.

I'm on a bed.

I crack an eye open and light streams in from the bathroom door that adjoins to the bedroom I'm in. Pipes squeak when someone turns off the shower. My limbs are heavy. Whatever they gave me is different than what I've had in the past.

I feel as though I'm paralyzed.

Panic skitters through me when a dark shadow fills the doorway.

Esteban.

He drops the towel that's wrapped around his waist and saunters toward the bed. I attempt to roll away from him but my body refuses to move. Hell, I can barely keep my eyes open.

"You must not forget who you belong to," he bites out as he fumbles around in the bedside drawer. He pulls out a condom and leaves the drawer sitting wide open. I can't look away as he rips open the foil and rolls the rubber down his cock.

The bed dips as he joins me. I can't move, so he manhandles my body so that my legs are spread wide open. My heart races so fast I think it'll explode at any minute.

Please don't.

My thoughts don't leave my mouth. They stay locked up inside my head. I beg him with my eyes, but I'm ignored.

"Don't worry," he assures me. "I'll lube you up so it doesn't hurt." He spits into his hand and then rubs his cock with it.

I want to close my eyes, but since they're the only things apparently working right now, I simply stare at him. He grips his cock as he pushes into me. I can feel the pressure but that's it. I've had sex with Esteban enough times to know that by the look of bliss on his face, he's deep inside me.

Anger surges within me and I glare at him. He doesn't notice.

Thrust after thrust, he takes what he wants, but I don't enjoy it this time.

If I was confused before, I certainly am not now.

Esteban is evil. Always has been. To think I thought he actually loved me in some fucked up way. Stupid girl. Hate for this man claws at me from the inside out. I'm nothing but an object to shove his dick into.

One day, when I'm not immobile, I will figure out a way

to make him pay for this.

"You're mine," he hisses. "Mine."

Over and over again he reminds me of this as he fucks me.

I am nobody's.

The closer he gets to orgasm, the angrier he seems to get. His palm finds my throat and he grips it so tight that the corners of my vision begin to darken. Nothing can be heard aside from his furious grunts and my ragged hisses of breath.

I black out completely.

When I come to, it's because I hear Oscar shouting at Esteban in the other room.

"Where are you going?" Oscar demands.

"I need to take a fucking walk to clear my head," Esteban snarls back.

The windows in the house rattle when he slams the door behind him. My heart is thundering in my chest and seems loud compared to the sudden silence. But then footsteps creak down the hallway. I can't see him but I feel his presence.

Help me, Oscar.

He hit me. Right in the face. Twice. But I could almost forgive him for that if he'd get me out of this mess.

Why did you hit me, Oscar?

That question plays over and over again in my head.

"Oh, Vee," he murmurs as he grabs something from the drawer. "We'll have to make this quick."

I want to ask him what he means, but then I hear his zipper go down and the familiar tear of a foil packet. I'm screaming inside for him to snap out of whatever shit he's going through. This is not Oscar. This is not the boy I've chased after since I was five years old. He rounds the side of the bed and climbs on to join me. His brows are furled together in concentration as he pushes my knees apart.

I try to meet his gaze, but he won't look at me. Instead, his focus is on his cock. More pressure within me. Some feeling is coming back. I know I'll be sore after this.

Please stop.

Nobody hears me.

Nobody fucking hears me.

He grabs the front of my dress and yanks it down to free one of my breasts. His mouth latches on to it. I can't feel it but I can hear the slurping sounds as he sucks on my flesh. A hard thrust slides me farther up the bed and a loud bang resounds.

Bang! Bang! Bang!

With each brutal thrust, my head slams against the headboard. Since some of my feeling is coming back, a thundering inside my skull begins to take hold. My vision blurs from being jarred by the repeated hits.

"Fuck," he murmurs, his eyes are wide, black and unfamiliar as an animal takes over. "I knew you'd feel fucking amazing."

I check out.

I can't stare at someone who I thought I loved while they rape me as if I'm nothing more than a toy to be used and abused. Our history. Our friendship. Our bond. Gone in an instant.

Despite my numb state, the fire within me is beginning to roar. It intensifies with each breath I take.

I'm going to kill them.

Both of them.

"Yes," he grunts, his movement jerky and out of control. "Fuck yes!"

I glare at him. Our eyes eventually meet. Guilt flashes in his dark brown orbs.

"Vee…" he trails off and clenches his jaw.

"Y-You—" My voice is but a whisper but at least it's working. I start to try to scream but his palm slaps over my mouth.

"Shhh," he hisses, his thrusting harder than before. Conflict is written all over his face but the animal bucking into me seems to win. "Shhhh."

I send him the nastiest hate-filled stare I can muster, but he's once again not making eye contact. Beads of sweat form on his forehead as he concentrates on his brutality. I guess keeping the Oscar I thought I knew so well buried while this thing takes over is hard work. He lets out a grunt and his body stiffens. Then, as if his pants are on fire, he yanks out of me and lets go of my mouth. He all but runs to the bathroom, and soon the toilet flushes. When he reemerges, his clothes have been righted and he's running a nervous hand through his hair.

"Y-You…" I whisper out, the accusation thick in the one word.

He shoves his hand into his pocket and quickly retrieves a pill. Then, he's striding over to me. The pill is pushed past my tongue and he forces it down my throat.

"Sleep now, Vee." His eyes darken as he leans forward and kisses my forehead. "This was all a dream."

I close my eyes because I can't look at him any longer. He's killed something that could have been beautiful. With this one single act, he's poured a lifetime of love down the drain.

This wasn't a dream.

It was a nightmare.

And when I wake up from it, I will make him pay.

Everything is blurry and confusing.

I can tell I'm in a car by the way it bounces along gravel and the sound of the engine loud in my ears. When I go to move my hands, I attempt to cry out upon noticing they're bound behind me. Tape covers my mouth, preventing me from making much noise. I'm hurting badly. Every muscle in my body aches. Bruises. Cuts. Hell, I may even have a broken rib judging from the way one side of me feels as though I'm on fire.

The plan.

Diego wouldn't be suspicious because they had *this* plan. Drop me off on the enemy's doorstep bloodied, raped, and beaten. Deliver me as a broken pawn that the cartel king can use to his advantage.

I've never hurt so much in my life. What concerns me most is the ache between my legs. Did they fuck me more while I was unconscious?

Tears should be falling yet they don't.

I'm fucking pissed.

My thoughts dissipate when the vehicle stops. Soon, the trunk opens, and Esteban appears in front of me. He grabs my elbow and hefts me out. His eyes are positively manic. There's no reaching the man who sometimes showed me some degree of humanity. The monster has been unleashed.

"Kill him and then you can come back home to me," he snarls against my ear as he roughly cups me between my legs. "Don't worry, I fucked you one last time so you'd stink of me when you meet that motherfucker."

I jerk my head to meet his gaze. The movement causes the dark night to spin around me due to whatever drugs he forced upon me. But when it slows back down and I lock onto his monstrous eyes, I send him a message of my own.

I'll kill him and then I'll come back to kill you too.

He must receive my message loud and clear because he fucking head butts me.

Can this night get any worse?

I'm thinking about how the night has only just begun when my world once again fades to black…

PART TWO:

"Criminal" by Fiona Apple

IV | Diego

"**C**LAUDIA AND CARMEN ARE DESTROYING THE LIBRARY," Jorge, one of my best men, announces. He's dressed neatly in a suit, but I know he's packing at least seven weapons under the fabric. Weapons meant to protect me. Not that I necessarily need protection, but when you have an entire country under your thumb, you tend to develop enemies along the way and unfortunately it becomes a necessity. I might be able to take them on one by one, but in the event they all come at me at once, I'd be fucked. So I suppose I do need Jorge and my men.

I exhale a puff of cigar smoke and arch an eyebrow at him. "Thank you for the warning, chico. I won't go into the library."

His jaw clenches in annoyance. "No, sir," he groans. "What do you want me to do about your wives?"

Only two out of my five women at war seems like a good day. About a year ago, my dick said, *let's have five wives*, against my brain's wishes. Now my dick takes back his goddamned words. They're all pissing me the fuck off. Pussy on demand had seemed like a grand idea back then, but of course it has supremely backfired on me. I should bring both Claudia and Carmen, wives number three and four, in here to fight over my cock since they're both in a bitchy mood. But then I'd have to look at them. Both are similar in appearance with their thick dark manes and olive-colored skin. Both bitches have the biggest fucking mouths in this country. I thought those mouths would be good for sucking cock. The problem is the other twenty-three hours of the day when they don't have a dick stuffed in their mouths.

"Get rid of them," I grumble and take another puff of my cigar.

He pulls a knife from his belt, and I shake my head.

"I didn't mean fucking off them, Jorge. I meant make them go away."

I pinch the bridge of my nose and will the tension to leave my shoulders. Everything is so goddamned complicated lately.

"You're not technically married to any of them. You don't owe them anything," he mumbles as he sheathes his knife.

"Fine. Send them away." Send them away forever.

"Even Olga?" he questions, a brief flash of hurt in his normally hard gaze. It's then I realize he's been fucking wife number two.

I meet his eyes with a glare. "Make her go away too. Even if it is to your bungalow. I don't give a fuck anymore. This was supposed to be for my benefit. They're worse than goddamned children."

"Martha and Rosa?" he questions.

Even though wives numbered in my head as five and six

are the least problematic, they're both on the fucking needy side. If Rosa begs for a baby one more time, I'm going to force Jorge to knock her up.

"Gone. Give them money. Lots of it. Just make them leave," I snap and then crack my neck. "I have enough shit to worry about right now. In case you didn't notice, our territory has quadrupled since Camilo is no longer a factor."

He gives me a clipped nod. "Are they to leave indefinitely, sir?"

"Until the next time I need my goddamned dick sucked," I seethe. "Do I need to make you a fucking spreadsheet? Get them out of my damn presence before I send you packing along with them!"

My chest heaves with exertion. I bring a hand shaking with anger back to my mouth and suck more of the sweet cigar smoke into my lungs. Closing my eyes, I lean back in the leather chair in my office and tilt my head up to the ceiling. This new place doesn't feel like a home at all. It's massive and cold. Fitting for that bastard Camilo. I'd only wanted to live in it to prove who the winner truly was. He may have won a few battles along the way, but I'm the motherfucker sitting in his chair now. This is my kingdom. Camilo is nothing but a corpse rotting away in a metal container back in the States.

The smile on my face falls as thoughts of my mother filter into my head. She'd always been religious and spoke of angels and demons often. Especially near the end when she teetered the line between life and death. Back when I'd desperately tried to scrounge together money for medicines to help her. I was sure I could cure her ailments. It wasn't until I'd had a near death experience myself on one of my missions for her that I believed in her words. That day, as my life drained from me, I met both an angel and a demon.

I spent my entire life prowling the shadows just waiting for that demon. To eradicate him from this earth. If it weren't for him cutting me to within inches of my own life, I'd have been able to kiss my mother as she passed on from this world to the next. Instead, I was laid up in a hospital bed and kept breathing by machines. When I was finally released, she was gone. I missed her death, her funeral, everything. That demon had to pay. And he did.

Now, to find that angel…

"Diego!" Jorge bellows as he stalks back into my office. "We have a problem—"

"JUST MAKE THE CUNTS LEAVE BEFORE I LOSE MY TEMPER!" I roar back at him and slam my fist on the mahogany desk.

He doesn't flinch and switches to English. "The women are packing. Not a problem. This problem is that there is a vehicle on the perimeter."

I stiffen. "Do we know who it is?"

"No. Luis and Manuel have ridden ahead to check it out. I'm going to meet them out there."

I rise and snag my Glock from the desk. "I'm coming with you."

"Sir, you shouldn't come out there in case it is a threat."

I tuck the gun into the back of my pants beneath my suit jacket and toss the cigar into the ashtray. "I dare them to threaten me. I need to release some steam. What better way than to slice up a few motherfuckers." I pat the knife that's sheathed at my belt. "Let's go."

He grumbles but doesn't argue the fact any further. I stalk ahead of him down through the long hallways. Until

I'm intercepted by Claudia.

"You can't make us leave!" she screeches and bares her teeth at me. "You promised to take care of us!" She starts screaming at me in Spanish and throws a vase my way. I duck and growl at her.

"I did take care of you until you got on my last fucking nerve. Now you'll leave in one piece or I'll slice you up and feed you to the pigs out back. Your decision, *Three*," I snarl. Her eyes narrow at my calling her by her number. They all fucking hate that, but I don't give a rat's ass. How else am I supposed to tell them apart? "Take the money and leave or try my patience. My blade is thirsty." I give her a wink.

"You prick!"

Ignoring her, I storm away to let someone else deal with her shit. Jorge gets held up for a minute but soon joins me outside. He wears claw marks down the side of his face. Better him than me.

We climb into his vehicle and haul ass along the gravel drive. Soon, the headlights reveal two men standing over a crumpled form. Looks like my men already eradicated the threat. As soon as the car stops, I climb out and stalk over to them.

"What is this?" I snap as I push past them.

"This was delivered a few minutes ago," Luis says, his tone gruff.

"With this note," Manual finishes and hands me a letter.

The cunt was a traitor. Thought she'd fit in quite well here. You're welcome.

The letter isn't signed. Fucking pussies. I dare them to speak these things to my face. With a growl, I squat beside the woman. Her hair is matted with blood. A once yellow dress is torn and dirty. Creamy white flesh is slightly blue from the cool temps and mottled with bruises all over. Small cuts dot her skin, making me cringe. I absently stroke the scars on my face.

"Bring her inside," I bark out.

"What? What if it's a trick?" Jorge questions.

"I don't give a goddamn!" I snarl as I rise to my feet. "She's a woman, and we're not leaving her here to fucking rot. Bring her inside and call for the doctor. We'll sort out the rest in the morning."

Jorge gives me a clipped nod before he scoops her into his arms. Her dress is torn down the front and her breast is bared to me and my men. Fury surges through my veins. I shrug out of my jacket and cover her before drawing her into my own arms. Jorge shoots me a questioning look, but I don't answer him as I stride back to the vehicle. I sit inside with her nestled against me in my lap. Dark red hair is covering her face. She can't be more than eighteen or nineteen years old as far as I can tell. When her head lolls back, I notice tape covering her mouth.

"Who is she?" Jorge questions as he starts the car.

"I don't know." *Sorry, ángel, but this is going to hurt.* I rip the duct tape away from her mouth. A small moan escapes her, and her lashes flutter from behind her hair but she doesn't reopen them. "But whoever pulled this shit is going to meet my goddamned blade."

Jorge wisely doesn't say a word in protest at my harsh declaration. Women seem to claw their way inside my heart and latch on to any sliver of vulnerability I possess. They get under my skin with their softness and sweet voices. And so help me when one is in distress, I want to be the motherfucking knight to swoop in and save her. Like little Gabriella Rojas. That girl was sweet yet feisty. In way the fuck over her head and in dire need of protection. Those boys in her life can't look after her. She's lucky I'm weak for the female sex. Any other cartel fuck would have put a bullet in her skull the day she tried to make professional business deals with monsters. But the girl had amused me.

Fucking women.

That's my problem.

It's why I have five wives. Of course they're not legitimate wives. I'd die before I so carelessly married a woman in God's eyes and tied myself to her in every way. My mother married my father. He was the love of her life until he was shot in an alley one day when I was three. I'd never disrespect her, dead or not, by marrying without love. My "wives" are more like steady girlfriends. Permanent pains in my ass.

I smirk as we pull into the drive. Not so permanent. By morning, my home will be quiet. Free from catty-ass cunts. I look down at the girl in my arms. Except for this one. This one is going to get better and then she and I are going to have a long talk. I need to know how a young woman like her ends up beaten and abandoned in a cartel king's driveway. There's a story. Daddy Diego loves a good bedtime story.

I'm sitting in the leather chair in my office when Dr. Tatiana Morales walks in. She'd been the surgeon when I'd nearly lost my life. It wasn't until I made something of myself that I was able to hire her to be my full-time doctor, earning double what she did at the hospital. Tatiana held me when I sobbed in my bed upon learning of my mother's death. She's seen me at my weakest and she's the closest thing I have to family.

"You're looking tired, hijo mío," she says as she sits across from me. She waves away the cigar smoke. "Bad habit," she chides and leans forward to snuff out my cigar that's sitting in the ashtray.

I smirk and shrug my shoulders. "I'm sure I have much worse habits."

She purses her lips, and it reminds me of my mother so much it hurts. "Speaking of your ruthless ways, I want to talk about the girl."

Jolting upright, I lean forward and frown. "What are her injuries?"

Sadness washes over her features. "Her wounds aren't consistent with a struggle, but I think it's because she was drugged. I'm not sure what was given to her, but she's still quite out of it. There was some vaginal irritation. My gut tells me she was raped."

Rage burns through my veins, and I fist my hands. "Anything else?"

She sighs and switches to English. "Most of the wounds are superficial. The one on her eyebrow required a couple of stitches, though." Her gaze falls to her lap. "Diego, she was severely malnourished. Her weight is at least fifteen pounds below what someone her age and height should be. The bones of her ribs protrude. She reminds me of an anorexic patient I had once."

Starvation. I know plenty about this. My mother often struggled to feed us when I was a young child. It wasn't until I hit my early teenage years that I had the wit about me to steal food for us. Hunger is a pain much worse than that of a knife. It's deep and consumes you to your soul.

"I'll make sure she's fed," I bite out. "Is that all?"

"I've tested for STDs and pregnancy. She's clear."

"How long until she's able to talk?" I ask, suddenly feeling sick to my stomach.

"I went ahead and started an IV with fluids. I'll watch her overnight. By morning, most of that should be cleared from her system. She'll need to be fed and taken care of," she tells me. Her brown eyes meet mine and her gaze hardens. "If you want me to take her to a woman's shelter in the morning, I will." I understand the look in her eyes. A look that says, *don't take advantage of her*. A look that tells me the girl has been through enough already.

"She stays here. She won't be harmed," I vow. And that's the goddamned truth. But the assholes who brought her here, I will gut without a second thought.

"Get some rest, Diego. You're exhausted."

I give her a nod and watch her leave my office.

Tomorrow, I will get some answers.

V | Vee

I WAKE WITH A START, A GNAWING HUNGER PAIN CLUTCHING at my belly from the inside out. Bright sunshine pours in from a window, and I squint against it as I sit up.

"Good morning, little one," a woman says.

I find an older Hispanic woman smiling at me. Kindness shines in her eyes. Am I in a hospital? My brows scrunch up in confusion.

"You're safe now," she assures me as she reaches for my hand.

I look down to see that I'm attached to an IV. She sets to removing the needle and then bandages me up.

"W-Where am I?" I croak out. Pain assaults me from every direction, but I power through it to find out where I am.

"You're under Diego Gomez's protection now." The way she says his name is one of fondness. I can't help but shudder, though. I'm in the beast's lair. When my eyes focus on the room around me, I recognize it as the very one I used to stay in whenever we'd come to visit the Rojas family all those years ago.

"I, uh, I…" Panic shoots through me. I'm here. I'm supposed to kill this scary dude and then I can escape.

Back to Esteban?

I choke back bile. He fucking head butted me. And worse yet, he and his brother sent me here as a pawn. They drugged and raped me. Disgust is quickly squashed by anger. How dare they use me!

"Are you hungry, sweetheart?"

And just like that, my anger is snuffed out.

"I'm starving," I whisper.

"Let's get you dressed and then we'll go down to breakfast. Ingrid is making homemade waffles this morning," she tells me with a gentle smile.

I'm confused. I'd expected monsters and mayhem. Not motherly smiles and hospitality.

After a slew of embarrassing moments during which I needed this stranger to help me pee and then dress, I eventually make my way down the familiar hallways on shaky legs.

"I'm Tatiana," she tells me as we shuffle along the corridor.

"Vee."

We settle at a table—the same table I used to eat at every summer with three Colombian boys. Now, I sit with Tatiana. She watches me carefully as the old lady who has to be pushing eighty waddles in, plopping plates down in front of us. I feel like an animal as I dive into the food. I've eaten nothing but sandwiches and soup for months. One bite of the waffles, and I feel like perhaps I died in that car last night. This has to be heaven.

I stuff myself to the point of pain at breakfast. And yet, I still have the desire to push more food into the pockets of the lounge pants I'm wearing. Just in case.

"You're welcome to come eat whenever you're hungry," Tatiana tells me with a smile. "I'll also make sure we put some snacks in your room."

My shoulders relax. I keep waiting for something horrible to happen. When we finish, she guides me back to my room. I stand awkwardly as I wait to be told what to do next.

"Books are over there. Television. Bathroom is in there if you'd like to bathe. I'll go into town later and pick you up more clothes. Would you like a swimsuit? It's hot out there, so maybe you'd like to swim. Swimming is a great strength builder." She babbles her words as though she's nervous.

I jerk my head over to her. "Thank you. Umm…sure. A swimsuit would be nice." I force a smile but can't help thinking about all the times Oscar and I would swim together. Back when we were friends. Back when he wasn't a vengeful prick. I mean, the rape and beatings make sense for their plan. Send me here as a victim. What they didn't realize, though, is that they created another enemy in the process.

Nobody fucks with the queen.

I'll get rid of this Diego asshole and then figure out a way to make the Rojas brothers pay for what they did to me.

"Don't be afraid of him," she mutters from behind me.

I freeze at her words. "I'm not afraid of him. I'm not afraid of anyone." My gaze drifts to hers, and I pin her with a glare. "I'm not."

She blinks at me in shock. "Good. That's good."

Tatiana slips out of my room. I walk over to the bookshelf. It takes everything in me to pull down the book I know holds pictures inside. All of the décor is the same as it was when I was here all those summers. Pulling *The Count of Monte Cristo* from the shelf, I settle into a chair by the window and open it. In the middle are a stack of Polaroids. Each picture is either of me or Oscar. We're making silly faces in each pose. In the last pic, we smartened up and stood in front of a mirror to get us both in the picture. In the photo, I'm fourteen and looking up at his lanky self. Love shines from my eyes and smile. He smirks at the mirror with one of his looks that got him more girlfriends than he knew what to do with. The only girlfriend it didn't get him was me. And it wasn't for lack of trying. That summer, I tried everything to get him to fall for me. I even swam nude in the pool for him. Nothing ever worked.

I grit my teeth and tear each photo of him in half. The pieces of the pictures flutter to my lap. With a sound of disgust, I swipe them all onto the floor along with the book. Then, I limp over to the bathroom. It's stocked with girly stuff. Hairbrushes, perfume, makeup. I can't help but become giddy over seeing such silly items. But these are simple items I've been denied for months.

A burst of fury explodes inside of me. Part of me wants to rage and push all of the pretty things to the floor with a clatter.

But then I remember *my* plan.

My plan is to destroy them all.

I stare in the mirror and hardly recognize myself. My hair has been blown into soft red waves, and I'm wearing clothes.

The dress is loose, but I love how the green is almost the exact shade of my eyes. I look like Poison Ivy from the *Batman* movies. Except I'm not trying to kill any good guys. I prefer the bad ones.

There is a basket full of unopened makeup, but most of it was meant for darker skin tones. I open a tube of mascara and brush some on my lashes and then opt for some lip gloss. Other than that, my bruises and cuts are on full display. I can even see the small dusting of freckles on my cheeks. At one time, I did everything in my power to hide them.

Now, I don't care.

The woman staring back at me is poisonous and vicious. She's not a victim or a delicate flower. This woman has thorns and deadly venom. This woman has a plan to hurt them all.

I smack my lips together before spritzing on some perfume and exiting the bathroom. I'm stopped dead in my tracks by the sight of a man wearing a suit on the other side of my bed, his back turned to me. He's staring at one of the halves of the pictures I'd torn up and holds the book in his other hand. In my moment of fury, I'd torn them all up and hadn't bothered to clean up the mess. Of course now, this implicates me as being somehow tied to the Rojas family.

"Jorge warned me this was a trick," the deep voice rumbles.

I'm stunned frozen. The man is much bigger than me. Broad shouldered with messily styled black hair on top of his head. He exudes strength and power.

"Diego Gomez?"

He turns to the side, and I get a brief look at his profile before he turns to shove the book into the empty spot it came from. I'd expected an old man like Camilo. Not someone closer to Esteban's age.

"I am," he states in a cold tone. "What's your name, ángel?"

He turns around fully to face me. The bed is between us and it seems like such a small obstacle between a cartel king and his captive. But I'm nobody's victim. Not anymore. Bravely, I tilt my chin and let my gaze bore into the lightest brown eyes I have ever seen. His eyes, not him, are the ones holding me captive as I momentarily get lost in them.

"Name," he grits out through clenched teeth.

I tear my gaze from its locked position on his eyes and study his face. Tiny silvery white scars crisscross all over his flesh. His cheeks are dusted with dark hair, thicker around his mouth and chin in a half-grown goatee. It's as if at one time, he kept it neat, but then one day simply forgot to care anymore, giving him the appearance of a wild man barely contained in a neat suit. My eyes land on his lips. Pink and full. So soft for a villain.

"Vienna Berkley," I tell him boldly and meet his light brown-eyed stare. "Vee."

His gaze softens as a half-smile tugs at his lips. The bad guys aren't supposed to be so damn handsome. They're supposed to be scarred and ugly. Yet here this one is—scarred up something terrible—yet he is anything but ugly. "I've been looking for you, ángel."

I tilt my chin up and bite out my words. "Here I am. And I am not an angel."

This earns me a wide smile which reveals every pearly white tooth in his mouth. The smile makes his light brown eyes twinkle with delight. "I can see I'm going to have fun with you, mi diablita. So much fun."

"Touch me and you die," I bite out, my voice slightly wobbling.

He chuckles. "You Americans are so feisty. It makes Daddy Diego so fucking hard."

I snort and lift an eyebrow at him. "We Americans also make fun of assholes who talk about themselves in third person."

He shoves his hands into the pockets of his grey pants, part of a crisp three-piece suit and a perfectly tied, navy-blue tie. He prowls around the edge of the bed. My hackles rise but I refuse to take a step back. His voice rumbles right through me when he says, "Americans are so quick to judge. I'm a friend, not a foe."

I tense when he rounds my corner of the bed. His movements are quick and stealthy. Like a jungle cat. In a matter of seconds, he's looming over me and toying with a lock of my hair. He brings it to his nose and he inhales me.

"Why are you here, Vienna?"

I turn to face him, refusing to cower under his intimidation. I've spent months cowering. This Diego prick is nothing in comparison to motherfucking Esteban. "Because they decided to hurt and betray me. Because they don't care about me. I'm here because they think I'm a pawn. I'm here because they don't know me at all."

"Fearless," he murmurs, his face inches from mine. I can smell the lingering scent of cigar smoke from this proximity.

"And angry," I admit, a slight crack to my voice.

His fingertip strokes my cheek. The movement is gentle and far from sexual, despite his earlier threatening words. "You want vengeance."

I swallow when his finger slides down the side of my

throat. "That's part of the plan."

Our eyes lock and a storm brews in his eyes. "What's the other part of the plan?"

"I like to call it plan D."

His loud, abrupt laughter startles me. "Ahhh, you are too fucking adorable. I like you."

I growl after him as he strides to the door, his long legs eating up the distance in no time. "Well I don't like you!"

He twists the knob and looks over his shoulder at me. "Not yet, mi diablita, but you will. All women like me eventually." With a wink, he's gone. And I refuse to admit that his stupid wink made my stomach do a little twist.

I manage to hide out in my room for the next few days. Ingrid brings me food fit for a queen—actual feasts, God bless her—and Tatiana takes care of me in other ways. She fusses over my well-being and brings me gifts. Once she took out my stitches, she brought me some makeup that matched my skin tone and some clothes that were my size. The swimsuit she purchased is a sparkly green two-piece that I absolutely love. I'm not sure what I'm doing here in Diego's house or exactly what my plan is—despite my lie, telling him I had one—but one thing's for sure, I'm going to swim in that pool. I may as well enjoy myself before I go on a bad-guy killing spree.

I haven't seen Diego since he came into my room that day, thank God. I never dreamed he'd be as hot as he is. Not that it matters. But it does make the plan easier. Whatever the plan is. As I put on the new swimsuit, I ponder what the plan really could be. I could always manipulate Diego into liking me. If I earned his trust, then he could send his men after Esteban and Oscar. He could do the dirty work. Then, I could take him out while he sleeps one night.

That plan seems feasible.

But getting men to like me has always backfired on me. The one man I'd always wanted never once touched me until he decided to use me in a ploy for revenge. Punched me in the damn face as if our friendship meant nothing and then raped me, knowing I couldn't stop him. A normal woman would be reduced to tears. Not me, though. I'm positively fucking furious. The Rojas brothers once again used me for their own personal gain. This is no different than all those summers when Oscar would toy with my emotions and Esteban would laugh at my expense. Their family has always been number one, and I was never a part of it. I was nothing but a silly girl to them.

They are going to regret this.

I'm going to need to make this plan work.

It's time to show them they fucked with the wrong chick. I'm not playing their games anymore. This time, I'm running the show. This time, I'll be the one laughing as I make them pay.

I twist my wild red locks into a messy bun. I've spent some time on my makeup today and given myself a darker look than I normally wear. I decide I resemble a seductress like Oscar claimed. Good. The cover up Tatiana brought me is cream-colored and sheer. I slip it on over the swimsuit before leaving the safety of my room. I'm heading toward the back staircase that leads to the pool when I hear a voice.

Curiosity gets the better of me, and I sneak down the hallway to Camilo's old office. When I peek around the doorway, I see Diego pacing the office with a phone pressed to his ear.

"She's fine, cariño. I promise on my big dick. Now take care of those babies. When have I ever not kept a promise to you?" He smiles. "That's what I thought." Then his voice grows serious. "Remember...you owe me big for this. And one day soon, I will call on you for repayment."

I'm dying to know who he is talking to. A wife? For some reason, that thought annoys me. A wife means more baggage. My plan to kill him will grow complicated with more people involved. He hangs up the phone and his eyes dart over to where I'm standing. His shit-eating grin falls away as anger contorts his features.

"Why in the fuck are you walking around the house in your bra and panties?" he snarls, the muscle in his neck twitching.

I curl my lip at him. "Good afternoon to you too, asshole."

His fury melts away and he grins. "That mouth will get you in trouble one day, mi diablita."

"I'm going swimming. Want to come?" I grit out. He's making my plans of seduction very difficult.

Shock flashes in his eyes and his mouth parts. I've only encountered him a couple of times and each time, I could easily read his emotions. I'd love to play poker with this guy. I would take him for every penny he's worth with that expressive face.

"You want me to come swim with you? With you..." he utters and waves at me. "Looking like that?"

I'm stung by his words. "Jesus! Be a prick, why don't you?

I thought I looked nice." My mouth forms a pout.

He stalks my way and looms over me without actually touching me. "You do not look nice."

I jerk away from him and storm toward the door. I've barely made it to the threshold when a strong hand grips my elbow. I'm forced up against the door jam, and Diego presses his entire hard body against me. His impressive erection stabs at me from behind. When he brings his mouth to my ear, his breath tickles me.

"*Nice* is a word for grandmas and fucking sunrises. You…" he murmurs as his palm roams around my front to touch my breast through my swimsuit. "You are like a thousand sunrises. Too bright and too goddamned beautiful for human eyes. I'm blind just looking at you, mi diablita."

His thumb rubs across my hardened nipple, and I gasp. So much for me being the seductress. The man pins me up against a doorframe and whispers a few sweet nothings into my ear and I'm seconds from begging him to strip me out of this *nice* swimsuit.

"I have too much work to do," he murmurs before nibbling at my earlobe. "But I can assure you, I'll be watching. I'll always be watching."

I shudder and it's not from disgust. I'm shocked that my body seems to respond to him whenever he's near. No fucking surprise there, though. My pussy seems to start flashing like a disco ball whenever a bad guy is in the vicinity.

Diego stalks off to somewhere in the house, and I stand there stunned for a moment. I'm really going to have to get my act together. Falling for the villain is not part of the plan. I've done enough of that to last a lifetime.

VI | Diego

THE SUN TODAY IS KILLER AND HOT AS HELL. I COULD BE inside in the air conditioning, working on shit, but instead, I'm standing on the deck staring at the redheaded vixen lying on a chaise lounge beside the pool. Her eyes are closed while one toe lazily swirls around in the sparkling pool water. Everything about her screams innocent and pure and fucking perfect. The best part about her is her rack. I swear those tits were hand sculpted by angels.

Speaking of angels...

I was given very direct orders by Gabriella Rojas not to touch her friend. When she found out Vienna was in my possession, she cried over the phone. It broke my heart a little to see the tough little thing reduced by her emotions. But when she asked to speak to her friend, I refused. I'm still certain the woman by my pool has an ulterior motive.

Until I figure out what that is, I'll play the girl's games. Clearly she's trying to get into my pants as part of her agenda. And I'd not be a gentleman if I didn't oblige.

I prowl silently over to where she bakes in the sun. The bruises still dot her flesh and small cuts remain. Despite her injuries, she's beautiful under the sun's rays. My hands crave to run my fingertips along her milky flesh, just to watch goose bumps form in their wake. She must have dozed off because she's fucking serene as she lies there without a care in the world. Her skin is slightly pink, and I know I'll need to make sure she stays covered so she won't burn.

"Mi diablita."

She cracks an eye at me and peers at me with her piercing green orb. "Mi motherfucker."

I snort and shadow her from the sun as I loom over her. "Where were you all those months?"

She bites on her pink bottom lip and the action makes my cock jolt in my slacks. "How do you know I was missing?"

"I know things."

A flash of sadness flickers in her eyes, followed by fear. She quickly chases it away with the fiery look she does so well. "Esteban Rojas took me. Held me captive."

I glare at her. Those hadn't been the words I'd expected to hear. Sure, they dumped her on my property, but I'd figured it was a one-time thing. "Did he hurt you often?"

Her nostrils flare. "When *didn't* he hurt me?"

"So you're here seeking asylum?" I don't understand her game.

Her eyes drift off behind me. She appears to be lost. "I don't really know what I'm doing." The honesty in her words is raw.

"I can keep you safe here," I assure her as I squat down beside her and twist a stray strand of red hair in my fingertips.

Her lips pull into a frown. "I've been told that a time or

two. You men are liars."

I give her hair a tug. "I'm not."

"Mmmm-hmmm."

"If I vow to keep you safe, I will keep you fucking safe. End of story," I growl.

She simply nods, but I can tell she doesn't believe me.

"After you dress, I want to have a little chat with you," I tell her as I release her hair and stand.

"What's there to talk about?" Her breasts jiggle as she heaves out a sigh. Those tits are too damn tempting.

"Everything," I murmur, dragging my gaze from her gorgeous rack. "Dinner. Seven. My office. Wear something sexy."

She hisses from her lounge chair, and I chuckle as I stride back toward the house.

"I'm not wearing anything sexy," she calls out after me.

"So don't wear anything at all," I say with a devilish grin and wink at her. "Such a naughty girl."

"You're disgusting."

I give her one last look and shrug before walking inside. I'll show her disgusting.

She walks through the darkness cloaked all in black. Her face is hidden from me. My fingertips twitch to pull the hood from her head, so I can see her. To see the angel who hides in shadows. But I'm bound. Bound and bleeding from a chair. Pain sears inside of me like never before and burns through my chest. She's somehow ripping me apart from the inside out. Maybe she's no angel at all.

A pale arm emerges from the dark clothing and points straight at me. The throbbing inside my chest intensifies. I feel as though the witch is trying to tear my heart right from my chest. She makes a motion with her finger. Down, starting from her left, and then up again to her right. It's a threat. I don't understand what she means but I know it's meant to hurt me.

I can't speak to her. My lips are sealed shut. I'm dying to plead with her to make the pain stop but I can't ask her anything. I am completely at her mercy.

"I could have killed you like five times," a sweet voice says, cutting through my nightmare.

I blink away the remnants of the dream and sit up in my chair abruptly. Apparently I passed the fuck out face first on my desk. Tatiana is right—I'm not sleeping well. These random catnaps throughout the day aren't cutting it.

"What time is it?" I grumble and swipe my fingers through my wrecked hair. My eyes finally dart over to find Vienna perched in a chair. She's wearing a dress that Claudia must have left behind. It's black and fitted. The low scoop neck reveals the full tops of her succulent tits while the short hem of the dress showcases her creamy thighs that now have a pink tinge to them.

"It's after eight," she murmurs. She fingers her messily styled red waves and arches an eyebrow at me. "I really could have killed you. But I didn't." Her lips quirk up into an amused grin.

I narrow my eyes at her and try to read the woman.

A few days ago, she showed up on my property raped and beaten to a bloody pulp. I discovered she has a past with the Rojas family but no longer seems tied to them. She's the same girl Gabriella had me locate. I'd expected a victimized woman who I'd need to nurse back to health. What I have sitting before me is no victim. I can practically see the wheels turning inside her head. Vengeance is in every smile and calculation in each glance. She all but admitted to using me for some personal gain. So fearless and bold.

"Come sit in Daddy Diego's lap," I utter in a low tone, my gaze once again traveling her milky thighs. "We need to discuss this little plan of yours."

A flash of annoyance flickers in her shimmering green eyes but she slowly rises. The dress fits her well, even if it is a little on the short side. She's artfully done her makeup in such a way that she looks much older than her young age. My cock thickens against my thigh as she saunters over to me, swaying her hips. Despite the makeup and the clothes, I sense her nervousness. It doesn't change the fact, though, that she's a natural seductress without even trying. The woman is an expert at drawing a man's eye and getting his dick to do all the thinking. Right now, as she sashays over to me, my head is clouded with thoughts of her and I tangled up under the sheets. It's been days now since the last time I got laid, something my cock reminds me of as it tries to escape my slacks.

When she rounds the desk, I roll the chair away and lean back in it. I point in front of me. "Sit there, mi diablita."

Her palms find the mahogany surface and she hoists herself on top of it. I smirk when she primly crosses her ankles. Rolling back toward her, I keep my legs spread apart and pin her shins with the front of my chair. With my eyes on hers, I take my time pulling a cigar from the drawer. She watches me as I take my father's old metal lighter and flick the lid open to produce a flame. I burn the end of the cigar until it's lit and then suck in the rich smoke. Camilo left these Cohiba Esplendido cigars for me as a parting gift. Unlike Tatiana, Vienna doesn't flinch when I blow the smoke up at her pretty face.

"Esteban kidnapped and raped you. And then you escaped?" I question as I take another puff.

Her brows crash together and she shakes her head. "Not exactly. He kept me for months. I thought I…" A frown tugs at her perfect lips. "I thought maybe he cared about me, but I later realized he'd been drugging me. I'd only recently come out of my stupor when he and his brother came up with the plan to send me here."

I stiffen at her words. "To kill me?"

A blush creeps up her slender neck and she nods. "But I told them I'd never killed anyone before. I didn't want to do it."

Anger bubbles up inside of me. "So you agreed to—"

"I agreed to nothing," she hisses, her gaze fiery enough to melt glaciers.

"So they kicked your ass, raped you, and dumped you on my lawn?" This makes no fucking sense.

The hardness leaves her expression, and she once again appears to be lost. This is the side of her that plucks at my heartstrings. I cannot deal with a vulnerable woman without wanting to tear the heads off of everyone who harmed her in her past.

"You forgot he also drugged me," she says with a dark

laugh. "But what I told you was true. They betrayed me."

I inhale another long drag of my cigar and scrutinize her. Hurt flashes in her eyes but she won't let it surface. She is fierce, this one.

"Why do they think you are so loyal to them? That you'll actually follow through with their plan after what they did to you?" I demand, taking another puff from my cigar. "Did they really assume you'd do their bidding and kill me? That you are even capable of killing me? Assuming you could, *why* would you?"

She uncrosses her ankles, and I can't help but drop my gaze to her thighs. The dress hides what lies beneath but it doesn't keep my stare from lingering there in hopes of catching a peek.

"I'm a good actress," she tells me, her voice but a whisper. "When I finally snapped out of my haze, I continued to play the part of broken, submissive woman. Esteban assumes I'll behave and follow his orders." She shudders. "I'm done being told what to do. I'm not ever going back to him."

We hold each other's gaze for a long while until her stomach grumbles. I tug the cigar away and lift an eyebrow at her. "You waited to eat dinner with me?"

Her nostrils flare. "You told me to."

"I thought you were done being told what to do," I challenge and run my knuckle along the inside of her knee.

Her body shivers at my touch, but she doesn't move away from me. "I need your help," she murmurs.

"You want them killed. And then what? I am to set you free?"

When her stomach growls before she can answer, I yank my phone from my breast pocket. I call down to the kitchen and bark out an order for them to deliver our food. Once I hang up, I lean back in my chair once again. The need to touch her is strong, but my cock muddies my brain. I need to think clearly for a moment.

"Mi diablita…"

"Yes." Her voice catches and for a split second she seems conflicted by her answer. Sadness flickers in her eyes. But then, her nostrils flare and she lifts her chin bravely. "I am no one to you, I know this. But I have money. I can pay you for your services."

What is it with these fucking adorable American beauties trying to make deals with me? I'm a bad man. A conqueror. Not some fair and just douchebag who is swayed by a pair of pretty tits and a shy smile. Oh…oh, wait. Perhaps I am that douchebag.

"I'm sure we can work something out," I grumble as I take a drag from my cigar. "But I don't want your money."

She narrows her glittering green eyes at me. "Well, I don't care. You're not doing it for free."

With my cigar between my teeth, I laugh and wink at her. "Oh, I want something in exchange." My gaze travels to her perfect rack. "I want something so very badly." When I finally look back up at her, she's not wearing a look of fear like her cute friend Gabriella did when we were making deals not so long ago. This girl is all fire and fury. The fucking devil in female form. Her red eyebrow that's recently been plucked to perfection is arched in a challenge. I'm pretty sure the look she's giving me is going to bring me to my knees one day. That look will be my demise.

"You want sex?" Her voice is hard, but it quivers ever so slightly. I notice it and latch on to her sliver of fear.

"I want sex," I agree as my knuckle teases her inner thigh again. "I want other things, too."

"Like what?" she murmurs, her bottom lip looking quite bitable right now.

"I'm not sure yet but I'll let you know."

She reaches forward, lowering her cleavage closer to my face and plucks my cigar from my teeth. I let out a groan when she slides into my lap and straddles my thighs. This girl is playing a dangerous game—a game she won't win. Not with me.

"You need me for more than sex," she tells me, her tone confident as she takes the most erotic drag from my cigar. The way her plump lips wrap around the tip has my cock aching for relief. Then, her fingertips are ghosting over the scars on my face. Her thumb slips into my mouth and she pulls it open.

I've pursued lots of women.

Women may be my weakness, but I'm really fucking good at showing them my strength.

I know what they want and I give it to them.

Seduction is my game.

Yet right now, this red-haired devil is playing my game better than I do. She exhales the cigar smoke into my mouth and brushes her lips against mine. I let out a hungry growl as I dig my fingertips into her hips.

"Be careful how you tread, mi diablita," I hiss, my hands barely staying under control.

"Or what?"

I snag her wrist and bring the cigar to my lips. "You might get in too deep. Don't forget that you're playing with fire here."

She grinds against my lap, causing me to hiss in pleasure. When her eyes meet mine, they're downright fucking evil. "I know all about fire, so trust me, I won't be the one who gets burned."

This bitch delivers threat after threat, and yet I'm gritting my teeth to keep from blowing my load in my pants. She's got my head all twisted up. This girl, who days ago, I fucking nursed to health, has morphed into this sultry demon hell-bent on bringing me down. Sure, she wants vengeance on the Rojas brothers. That much is clear.

But she also wants me.

Dead.

I can see it in her eyes.

Feel it in her murderous glares.

Hear it in her softly spoken threats.

And yet, here I am, indulging the succubus of a woman. I'm wondering how many times I'll get to fuck her before she delivers that fatal blow when I least expect it. Leaning forward, I drag my nose along the bare part of her tit, peeking over the top of her dress. She lets out a gasp that has me grinning wolfishly.

"Well, Vienna," I murmur against her flesh. "Looks like you've made yourself a deal. I'll bring down the bastards who hurt you and then I'll bring you down to your knees where you'll suck my fat cock until you're blue in the face."

She sucks in a deep breath and leans away from me. Her lips are parted while her eyes are lit up like green flames. Hot with desire. On fire with lust.

"We have ourselves a deal, mi diablita?" I question as I take the cigar from her fingertips. "You for them?"

"Deal."

VII | Vee

Plan D is in full effect. I hide my smirk as I slide off the desk the moment a young man rolls in a cart of food. He wants to have sex with me in exchange for killing Esteban and Oscar. It's almost too easy. Sex with a man like him would be kind of like a bonus, certainly not a chore. So I'll bang Diego and then bolt. Win, win. At one point, I thought I wanted him dead too, but things change. He'll make a better partner alive.

"Where are you going?" he questions, his voice low yet amused.

"I thought we were going to eat." My tone is pouty, and I instantly hate how transparent I am when it comes to food.

"We are," he growls. "But sit here."

He pats his thigh beside the hard length that is every bit visible through his slacks. Whatever he's packing in there looks dangerous. A big fat snake ready to strike. The cock he's hiding is what male porn stars only wish they had.

Knowing I need Diego to carry out my plan, I obey. I kick

off my heels and pad back over to him. The guy who brought our food is busy setting out the dishes on the desk without saying a word. I sit on Diego's powerful thigh and can't help but shiver. Do these Colombian men live on the regiment of sleep, fuck, and work out twenty-four hours a day?

I'm distracted by the man setting out the food. He places many different styles of dishes all over the surface that smell heavenly. I remember many of them from when I used to come visit. Dishes that are native to the country. My mouth waters for a taste.

"I'm not sleeping with you until you carry out your end of the bargain," I tell him as I snag a hot seasoned piece of meat from a bowl. Flavor explodes on my tongue when I pop the sliver of steak into my mouth. A groan of pleasure rumbles from me. "Oh, God, that's so good."

Diego chuckles and his fingers run circles along my back through the fabric of the dress. "Carne Guisada con zanahoria," he tells me, his voice friendly. "My mother's recipe. It tastes better with the carrot sauce."

He leans past me and spoons some of the orange-colored sauce onto the meat that's been cut thinly. With a fork, he scoops up a mound of it and brings it to my face. My eyes dart over to his, searching for malice, but I only find eagerness in his expression. He wants me to like this dish.

I part my lips and accept the bite he feeds me. Esteban fed me sandwiches and soup. At one time, I'd thought it was borderline romantic.

Then I woke up.

Then I realized he was fucking with my head.

"Oh," I murmur between chews. "That's really good. Did your mother make it?"

His black eyebrows crash together and he scowls. "No. She's dead."

I swallow the morsels before regarding him sadly. "Mine's dead too. Esteban drugged her with heroin like he drugged my friend Brie. When Esteban finally came back for us in the shipping container, it was too late. I was half starved to death and my mother had died from withdrawals."

His eyes dart all over me. He clenches his teeth and scoops up another bite. I expect him to feed himself, but he once again gives me the bite. It should annoy me or remind me of Esteban. But it actually doesn't bother me at all. The food is good and he's not as evil as I originally thought.

At least I hope not.

I tend to see the best in the bad guys. They dazzle me with their evil grins and their bad boy muscles, and I fall hopelessly at their feet where they tend to kick me while I'm down.

"My mother died of pancreatic cancer. One day she was fine and strong. The next day, she was weak and dying." His jaw clenches as he looks past me toward the wall. I follow his gaze to a painting. The woman in the picture is young and beautiful. Her dark hair is curled and pulled to one side. She smiles but her features are sad. I don't have to be told it's his mother, because I know. They look just alike.

"I'm sorry," I murmur, my eyebrows pinching together in pain. My mother was difficult and bitchy and unkind. It's my father who I loved unconditionally, despite his flaws and mistakes. I understand how it feels.

He grunts and stabs at more meat. Once again, he feeds me rather than himself. I can tell the talk about deceased mothers has soured his mood. A bad mood doesn't fare well with my need to keep him on my side. In order to keep the conversation light again, I pick up a different fork and poke at what looks like some shredded beef over rice. When I turn to look at him, he's still staring at the portrait.

"Open up." I flash him a smile before bringing the fork to his lips. "Partner."

He smirks but obeys. "Carne Desmechada o Ropa Vieja," he tells me after he swallows.

The rest of the meal carries on like this. I try many new dishes that I decide I very much love. After months and months of hardly any food at all with shit selection, dining with Diego feels like a royal feast.

"So you're the king of Colombia now?" I question.

He chuckles, the sound boyish in quality. My stupid heart stutters at the sound of it. "I suppose so," he agrees. "But if we're partners and I'm the king…" His light brown eyes flicker up to mine and he grins wide. A shiver races down my spine. "Then you're my queen."

I hold his stare despite my desire to look away. I think he's trying to intimidate me.

"I'm going to fuck you until those assholes are dead. That's my deal, mi diablita."

Mentally, I had hoped our deal just meant the one time. But deep down in my heart, I knew it would never be just once. "Whatever…" I trail off and reach forward to grab the knot of his tie. "Now?"

Surprise washes over his features, but then he hardens his expression. "When I want it, you will know. And when I come for it, you will give it to me."

I unknot his tie despite his words. "Are you going to force me?"

He grips my wrist in a painful way. "I've never had to

force a woman." His eyes darken a shade. "They all beg for Daddy Diego's cock."

The moment of seriousness is swiped away when I snort with laughter. And as soon as one giggle escapes, an eruption of them soon follow. I laugh until tears stream out. When I sneak a glance at *Daddy* Diego, he's glaring at me, which only serves to make me giggle harder.

Striking with the quickness of a snake, he jolts to his feet and twists me toward the desk. I cry out when he shoves me down on the hard surface. My hand smashes into a half eaten dish while my cheek gets pressed against what feels like dinner rolls. I cry out when he rubs against me through our clothes. His erection is giant and rock hard as it slides along the crack of my ass.

"You will beg for it," he snarls, his fingers tangling up in my hair.

He's furious, but I can't help but start to giggle again. My villain sensor is broken and I can't seem to turn off the part of me that provokes them. His grip on my hair becomes almost painful, and yet I continue to snort with laughter. I'm completely flattened against the food when he covers my body with his.

"Oh, Daddy Diego," I choke out through amused tears, "please give me your cock."

The man freezes behind me and then his chest starts to rumble. "What is wrong with you?" he grumbles against my hair near my ear. "I have you bent over my desk, with food staining your dress, with my angry anaconda pressed against your ass, and you're still laughing. Have you no fear, woman?"

"Angry anaconda?" I snort again but then I relax despite

the precarious position I'm in. "I haven't laughed in so long. I forgot what it truly felt like."

"I'm glad you're so amused," he bites out as he stands up, relieving me of his weight.

Carefully, I pull myself away from the desk. Plates clatter as I peel myself from them. When I look down, food is smeared all across the front of me.

"You're fucking filthy."

I stick my tongue out at him. "You made me this way."

His jaw clenches as he points toward the door. "Go get cleaned up and then meet me upstairs."

"What's upstairs?" I scrunch my nose up as I try to recall what's on the third floor. Last I remember, it was full of junk.

"You'll find out when you get there." His gaze falls to my breasts. "Dress comfortably."

Forty-five minutes later, my hair is clean and dried. The heavy makeup I had on before has been wiped away. He said to dress comfortably, so I'm standing in the bathroom staring at the white camisole and short silk shorts in the mirror, wondering if this is too comfortable.

The plan is to make him want me.

The plan is to make him kill them for me.

And per our agreement, I'm going to have to have sex with him. Lots of times, I'm sure. I meet my own green-eyed stare in the mirror. Dressed like this with no makeup, I look younger than my almost nineteen years of age. But the coy smile on my lips and the way my pink nipples show through my white shirt are far from innocent.

Esteban taught me that sex is animalistic and raw. Your mind shuts down as the nerves in your body take over. Pleasure exists where sanity cannot. It'll be just like it was with Esteban. I will turn off my mind and take pleasure in the deed.

Before I chicken out, I creep out of the bathroom and start for my bedroom door. The house is quiet. I know there are staff members and his men in different areas of the house, but right now they're being silent. I make my way down the dark hallways until I find the stairwell in the back. Hastily, I pound up the steps and push through the doorway at the top.

When I make my way through the door, I freeze.

Diego is no longer wearing a suit, looking dapper and distinguished as he usually does. No, right now he's looking kind of thuggish, dressed in a loose pair of holey jeans and a tight white wife beater. He's lean but muscular, like a fighter. Where Esteban is all bulk and strength, Diego seems more lithe and possesses a powerful grace.

I stare at him for longer than I should while his attention is on a gigantic television as he mashes buttons on the remote. Tattoos color his arms, and I can see more on his back through his shirt. Who knew all this was hiding under those suits.

"What are we doing?" I murmur, my gaze stalling at his beautifully curved shoulders. "I thought we were having sex."

He looks over his shoulder and his messy, now wet hair hangs in his eyes. I don't miss the smug grin on his face, though. "Patience, mi diablita. I'll sex you up when I am good and ready. It's all about the build up." When he turns back to the television, I let out a growl of annoyance.

"Patience isn't a quality I possess, mi motherfucker." I huff and storm over to him. "I'm not doing whatever this is." I motion around the media room. "Dates aren't part of the deal."

He slams the remote onto the entertainment table and snaps his gaze to me. It's in this moment, as his eyes flicker with fury, I remember I'm in the lion's den. I've negotiated with a monster to do monstrous deeds all in exchange for my monstrous goddamned pussy. A vein in his neck pulsates and his jaw ticks as he regards me. And then, much like the snake he can be, he strikes.

His palm curls around my throat and he pushes me until my back hits the wall. He doesn't squeeze my neck, but his eyes convey to me that he could choke me dead in a matter of seconds if he wanted to. I need to make sure he doesn't want to.

I press a palm to his solid chest over his heart and clutch his wrist with the other. He loosens his grip, letting me peel him away from me. But he doesn't back off. His body crowds mine until I'm sandwiched uncomfortably between him and the wall.

"This is why I don't have wives anymore," he grumbles, his hot breath inches from my face.

I stiffen, no longer concerned about being trapped by a cartel bad boy. "Wives? As in plural?"

"Yes, wives," he says simply. "Plural. Past tense."

Tilting my head up at him, I frown. "Pig."

His lips curl into a grin. "So you think I'm disgusting and gross. I'm still waiting to show you how nasty I can be, mi diablita."

My nostrils flare and I open my mouth to tell him where

he can stick that statement when he leans forward. His scent envelops me just a moment before his lips press against mine. The kiss is so sudden. So surprising. So…sweet. I'm stunned frozen. That is, until his palm curls around the side of my neck and he coaxes my mouth open with his tongue.

We both taste of toothpaste. I'm consumed by the way his tongue expertly dances with mine. Unrushed but deliberate. Soft but experienced. His thumb caresses my jaw and a whimper escapes me. I hate the vulnerable whine it carries. A sound that says I need his gentle touch more than I need air.

My fingers begin tugging at the bottom of his shirt, but he stops me with a growl. His hands find my wrists and he presses them against the wall above my head. This action makes my tits squeeze together.

"Sex," I whisper. "You…naked…"

He nips at my lip. "Not yet."

I want to argue, but his tongue is back in my mouth, owning me. He dizzies me with his kiss to the point that my knees buckle. My hands are released, and the next thing I know, I'm scooped into his arms. His lips are on mine again as he walks across the room. I'm tossed onto a comfy sectional sofa, but he doesn't join me.

"Want something to drink?" he questions as he saunters back over to the television.

"Are you kidding me right now?" I grumble. My body is trembling with desire over here, and I'm practically dripping with need. And he's playing hospitable host?

"I'll take that as a yes," he says with a chuckle.

I cross my arms over my chest and watch with irritation as he starts a movie and then begins digging around in a mini fridge. He grabs a couple of beers and pops the tabs. I accept one and down half of it as he flips off all the lights. Once it's dark, besides the glow from the television, he sits down beside me.

"What are you doing?" I question, annoyance in my tone.

He stretches his arm across the back of the sofa behind me and takes a pull from his beer. "I'm chilling the fuck out. What are you doing?"

I blink at him several times. "I don't know what to make of you."

He chuckles, and his gaze darkens. "Likewise. You're a pretty little puzzle I don't quite understand."

"But you're a big, badass cartel king who likes to fuck and kill," I snap.

He seems to consider this. "And you're a little girl with a big mouth who needs protection," he growls back.

I glare at him and grit my teeth. "So we're just going to pretend we aren't those people and have a sleepover?"

Amusement glitters in his eyes. "When was the last time you weren't stressed out about shit? When was the last time you just sat down, enjoyed a beer, and watched a movie?"

Forever. It's been forever. I think the last movie I watched was with Ren and Oscar at my apartment. That seems like ages ago. Back when life was simple and fun and hopeful.

Now life is dark and ugly.

"I'm not old enough to drink," I pout as I drain the rest of my bottle.

He regards me with a devilish grin. "And you're not in Kansas anymore, Dorothy. Here, under my roof, you can do whatever the fuck you want. Here, we live like kings." He winks. "Mi reina."

I set the bottle down and let his words simmer. I'm so wound up, violence and vengeance running through my veins, that I don't know if I can fully relax. But soon, we're both chuckling at the stupid movie with Channing Tatum and Jonah Hill who are cops and go undercover at a high school.

When the air conditioner kicks on, I shiver and burrow against Diego's warm body. He smells good. Clean and manly. Maybe for a night, I can pretend I'm just me. Vee.

His fingertips stroke the outside of my arm, and I am comforted by his soothing touches. It makes no sense. According to Esteban and Oscar, he's a violent man who killed Camilo.

Maybe he's a hero.

Camilo was certainly the bigger villain of the two.

I'm sure Mr. Rojas deserved it.

Soon, I fully relax and fall asleep in the arms of a supposed monster. I've slept in the arms of a real life monster. This supposed one doesn't feel so scary at all.

VIII | Diego

"**P**LEASE, SIT."

Jorge's features are hard as he folds his bulky frame into the chair across from my desk. Despite his impassive features, I can tell he's nervous. A slight dart of his nearly black eyes. A tick of his jaw. An impatient glance at his watch.

"I've made a deal," I tell him, my voice low. "With the devil it would seem."

Jorge relaxes his shoulders. "You make deals with devils all the time."

But this devil is far more dangerous than anyone I've encountered before.

"How is Olga?"

Once again, he stiffens. "I'm sure Olga is fine."

I lift an eyebrow at him. "Did you sleep with her while she lived under my roof?"

He grits his teeth and nods. "I did."

Most men would lie to a cartel king to spare their life.

Jorge is not a liar. He's extremely loyal—even if he did fuck one of my wives. She was weak—a habitual crier—and didn't even like anal. My loss is his gain. Good luck with that one, man.

"I should slit your throat for that," I growl. "Blatant disrespect."

His eyes narrow. "I would deserve it. Love makes you do unimaginable things, though. Stupid things."

"I wouldn't know," I bite out. "I'm not going to kill you, but we do need to get men out there hunting the remaining Rojas brothers. I want them brought to me alive."

"Do I need to know with whom you made this deal?" he questions.

I let out a sigh. "The girl. She's connected with the family. They wronged her, and she wants vengeance. And I…" I trail off and scrub at the scruff that's trying to grow in on my cheeks. "I want her."

"Another wife perhaps?"

I shrug and pick up a cigar. "I believe I'm done with wives for now."

He cracks a rare smile. "I'll believe that when pigs fly."

"Men. Rojas brothers. This week. Those are my orders," I grit out, ignoring his jab. "I also want Ricardo on the shipments going through Panama to get to Mexico. Tell him we—"

"I want to sit in on this meeting," Vienna interrupts from my office doorway. My gaze darts over to her like a heat-seeking missile. Last night, when she'd fallen asleep, I'd left her there despite my desire to strip and then fuck her. This morning, she's already showered and dressed. She's a picture of innocence in a knee-length white summer dress.

Her silky red hair has been loosely braided to one side and her makeup is minimal. To an outsider, she resembles an angel.

I'm no outsider.

"Good morning, mi diabliata," I greet with a wolfish grin as I visually feast on her cleavage.

"Morning, mi motherfucker," she chirps back. "What's on the villain agenda for the day? Are we skinning anyone alive?"

Jorge raises his eyebrows in surprise at how she speaks to me so disrespectfully. I smirk at him before gesturing for Vienna to come closer. She shows no hesitation, despite whom she's approaching, and bounces over to me.

"Sit," I instruct.

She eyes Jorge with apprehension but eventually sits on the edge of my desk, facing me. Our eyes meet and her green eyes flicker with curiosity when I pat the side of her leg. When she lifts it, I grab her ankle and place her bare foot on top of my thigh. Once she has both feet on my thighs, I lean back in my chair and admire her beauty. Unlike the Colombian women I'm used to, this one stands out with her pale, slightly freckled flesh, brilliant red hair, and the plumpest dick sucking lips I have ever seen. Her glittering green eyes dance between good and evil, just barely hugging the line.

"Now what? When do we kill them?"

Jorge snorts, and I can't help but smile at her. "So eager. And we haven't even had breakfast yet."

She shrugs and picks up my steaming mug of coffee. I regard her with lifted eyebrows as she drinks from my cup as though it's hers. I'm not sure why that gets my dick hard, but it does. Goddamn this vixen.

I grip the inside of her thigh just above her knee and caress the flesh. She sets the coffee down and attempts to draw her knees together. I grip her by the ankles and spread my thighs apart, which in turn spreads her open to me. With my eyes back on hers, I lift the hem of her dress and peek underneath.

"Red. I like it." My voice has dropped several octaves.

"Should I go?" Jorge asks.

"Stay. We have business to conduct. My *partner* here wants in on the details. So, Jorge, fill her in on your plans," I instruct as I let my palm roam up her thigh again. When my longest finger brushes against her panties, she lets out a sharp gasp.

"Jorge..."

"Uh, right. So, ma'am, we—"

"Call me Vee," she interrupts.

My hands rub against her in a teasing manner. I'm dying to take a look at her cunt. This little girl wants to play big games with big bad men. I'll let her play. I wonder how long it'll be until she throws in the towel.

While Jorge drones on about shipments and territory changes, I attempt to distract her. I can tell she's trying to listen, but it must be difficult for her when I keep rubbing my thumbs along the sensitive flesh of her thighs near her panties. She doesn't protest when I kiss the inside of her thigh near her knee. A soft little peck is all she gets at first. But then I catch whiff of her arousal. And now I'm hungry. I nip at her pale flesh and grin when it starts turning pink immediately.

"Why not go through Buenaventura?" she questions, looking over her shoulder at Jorge.

I perk up. "What about Buenaventura?"

"It was where Camilo sent shipments to my father's shipyard," she says, turning back to look at me. Her red brows are crushed together as she thinks. "If you took over his territories, why aren't you utilizing his shipyard? Are the U.S. monies not that much?"

I narrow my eyes at her. Brie had detailed out everything she knew, but she played dumb when it came to the specifics about where the Berkleys were concerned. I'd assumed we were at their shipyard when I gutted Camilo like a fucking fish, but I had to get my ass back to Colombia. I knew shipping product to the U.S. was a huge part of Camilo's profits, but I simply didn't have the connections he had. Berkley was dead and his daughter was missing. But now?

"How much do you know about your father's business?" I question.

Her green eyes sparkle. "I've followed him around since I was little girl. I used to sit in his office and play with my toys or color while he discussed business and made deals. For as long as I can remember, I tagged along with my dad. When I got older, he tried to keep me out of the limelight because he considered me to be a vulnerability that someone could use against him, but I was still curious. I knew how things worked. And I know that when I turned eighteen, Daddy made sure to add me to his accounts and properties. He didn't fully trust my mother and he wanted me to hurt for nothing if anything ever happened to him." Her eyes become glassy with unshed tears but she quickly blinks them away. "Something did happen to him. He was murdered. While I was locked away in that metal container at my father's shipyard, Esteban brought me paperwork. He wanted everything to run as seamless as before." She bites on her bottom lip for a moment to keep it from quivering. "I signed checks in exchange for food. I paid bills for water. I did whatever Esteban asked of me so that I could survive."

I've hated Esteban Rojas since I was a teenager. We'd been two fucked-up kids on opposite sides of the line that had been drawn in the sand. He was a cartel prince. I was a thief who was slowly stealing bits and pieces that would build my empire. The privileged son against the son born of poverty. Two sides of a coin. A lifetime of war.

Nothing compares to the hate I have festering for him inside my chest. The fact that he could hurt women disgusts me. Esteban acquired quite the reputation for being a monster. He'd cut out the tongue of a friend of his younger brother's. I'd seen him nearly get killed by a small-time cartel leader when he'd fucked around with his sister. The only reason Bolo spared Esteban's life was because everyone in Colombia answered to Camilo.

But Camilo is dead.

Nobody can protect Esteban anymore.

The sins of his past are going to hang him in the end.

And I'll be holding the motherfucking noose.

"You're willing to give it all to me?" I ask, my brow lifted in question.

This gorgeous little devil before me grins. "Oh, mi motherfucker, of course not. I'm simply telling you that you *have* to partner with me if you want your shit in the U.S. Exporting to Mexico isn't nearly as profitable of a way to get the cocaine over the border because you have to pay a middle man. You need to go straight to the source if you want to keep most of your profit." Her fingers toy with the hem of her dress and she slides it farther up her thighs distracting me for a moment. I flash her a warning glare until she stops fucking with her dress and continues talking. "Killing Esteban and Oscar is what we've made a deal for. Them for sex. Easy peasy. But Buenaventura to San Diego is a *new* deal. You need *me* to push the coke into the U.S. My father had contacts within the feds and local authorities. At one time, they'd been on to my father and Camilo, but then they married my adopted sister Brie off to Duvan. It was a legitimate marriage that bound our two countries in a way that had them off their backs."

"So what are you saying?" I demand, irritation bubbling inside me. I knew this bitch had ulterior motives.

"I'm saying," she purrs as her foot slides to where my cock is still hard in my slacks. She rubs against it with the bottom of her foot. "You need me. This partnership, if you will, can be bigger than just one transaction. It can be a union. A deal bound by law—"

"And God," I finish with a growl. "A wife."

Jorge snorts. "Would you look at that? I think there's a pig outside flying."

I clench my jaw and glare at her, but it's hard to stay pissed when she rubs at my cock with her foot.

"It's just business, *Daddy* Diego," she says in her most seductive voice.

The bitch is playing me. I'm staring right into her calculating green eyes and I can see right through her bullshit. Yet…I am weak.

Goddamn women.

"Why would you subject yourself to this world? Drugs. Mayhem. Murder. A little girl like you belongs on the other side of a white picket fence in suburbia. Not in the middle of

Colombia making deals with evil men. Why, Vienna?"

She leans forward and clutches my tie, pulling me closer to her. "Because I have nothing left. My legacy is all I have. It was my father's business and now it belongs to me. I won't hand it over to Esteban Rojas. And I certainly won't hand it off to you." Her voice becomes a whisper. "This is what I want, and you're going to give it to me."

I grab her hips and drag her into my lap. She lets out a yelp but settles herself against my throbbing cock. My palms slide under her dress so I can grab her ass that's covered by the silky panties I saw earlier.

"What if I just want to take it instead?" I demand as I yank the front of her dress down far enough to expose her nipple. "What if I just want to use you until I get what I want?" My mouth covers her pale pink nipple. I suck on the soft flesh until her nipple peaks and hardens. Then, I nibble on it. Her fingers thread into my hair and she whimpers.

Goddamn those whimpers.

"I'm going to go," Jorge states.

"No!" Vee and I both shout at the same time.

I jerk my gaze up to stare at her in confusion. "You like an audience?"

She rolls her eyes. "No, but I do like the idea of having a witness."

"Jorge is loyal to me. What makes you think he's a neutral factor here?" I'm amused by her implication.

Her green eyes darken as she eyes me cautiously. "You said you always make good on your promises. I'm simply making sure you'll remember we made such promises."

I narrow my eyes as I palm her tit through her dress. I'm looking for any weakness. Any sign that she can't handle what she's proposing. Her gorgeous face remains impassive. The girl is fire, and I want to get burned by her.

"You'd marry someone like me? For business?" I smirk and squeeze her tit through her dress.

"I'd wear your ring and all," she drawls with a fake southern U.S. accent as she bats her eyelashes.

I lean forward and inhale her sweet scent before eyeing her with a wicked stare. "If you married me, it would have to be binding and under the eyes of God for it to be legal. And if I take a *real* wife, under God, there is never any getting out of it. Ever."

"I understand," she says softly, a tiny twinge of fear in her voice.

"'Til death, mi diablita. The only way out is through the backdoor to hell. Do you understand?"

She swallows and levels me with a brave glint in her eyes. "I understand. The ultimate business partnership. What is mine becomes yours. And…" She clutches my tie at the knot and tugs me forward again. Her breath tickles my lips and my cock grows impossibly harder. "What's yours becomes *mine*. What was once theirs becomes *mine*. I'll be the queen of—"

"Everything."

I grip her neck and pull her to my mouth. Her kiss is hesitant at first but then she gives in to the slow tango of my tongue. I need the U.S. exports. It was such a huge facet of Camilo's territory. This partnership with little Vienna Berkley is a brilliant move. It further cuts the Rojas family. Esteban and Oscar may think they can regain what was theirs, but they are sadly mistaken. They are dead to this country. If they knew what was best for them, they'd leave while they still can. I may have promised Brie I wouldn't hurt Oscar back when I made my deal to protect her in exchange for information, but I didn't promise her that nobody else would. Colombia is mine. I am the king.

And Vienna wants to be my queen.

"Trust is a big thing for me," I growl. "I need to know you're not going to fuck me over the moment you get what you want."

"Sir—" Jorge starts, but I silence him with a wave of my hand.

"We'll sign a contract," she tells me as if that's the simplest idea in the world.

My wheels begin to turn. A contract is an excellent idea. But I want one written in blood. A constant fucking reminder.

"You're ready to be mine for life?" I question as I squeeze her thighs. I slip my palms under her dress and run my thumbs along the sides of her panties. She gasps and squirms. So responsive. I wonder what sort of sounds she makes when she comes.

"I'm ready to take what's mine. I'm tired of being kicked around and used. And if that means partnering with Diego Gomez in order to fuck over those who stole from me, then so be it."

"Sir—"

"It's done," I hiss to Jorge. "I've made my decision. Call Tatiana. I'll want her available tonight for what I have in mind. Get me a priest. This partnership begins tonight."

When he hesitates, I roar. "Go!"

Vienna doesn't flinch at my raised voice, but Jorge hustles from the room. Her eyes are on my face as she brushes her fingertips along my scars. "How'd you get these?"

"It doesn't matter," I snarl as I stand abruptly with her in my arms. Her eyes widen when I lie her back on my desk. "I want to celebrate our engagement."

She cracks a genuine smile that makes my heart thump. "I don't have a ring yet."

I push her dress up to her hips and begin sliding her red panties down her thighs. "I'll give you something better."

I sit back down in my chair as I toss her panties to the floor. Her cunt glistens with arousal. The tiny strip of red hair makes my mouth water for her.

What's one more wife?

But this one will be permanent…

The wife.

Wife number one. I never numbered any of my previous wives with that slot because I knew one day someone would fill it. Someone different and worthy.

I hope my mother isn't rolling over in her grave.

"Tell me no, mi diablita," I growl as I roll my chair forward so I can inhale her scent.

She sits up on her elbows and lifts a sculpted brow at me. "Why on earth would I ever do such a thing?" Her knees fall apart, inviting me. She bites on her bottom lip, her eyes heated with lust. "I want my gift, Daddy Diego."

My cock aches to slam into her. "You're a succubus aren't you? You were sent straight from hell to tempt me into giving up everything. So help me, if you fuck me over…" I trail off with a hiss.

"We both have a lot at stake here," she says softly. "I have nothing left except for my father's business. You're the only person who can help me hold on to that. Plus…"

I press a kiss to her sweet pussy. "You need protection."

Her breath hitches when I run my tongue along her seam. Sweet. This girl is so sweet and innocent despite her hard words.

"I can't be a prisoner again," she whispers.

I run my thumb along her opening as I tease her pink clit with my tongue. "Isn't that what marriage is? You'll be bound to me."

She reaches forward and grips my hair. Our eyes meet. Fire and determination and barely contained lust blaze in her glittery green orbs. "As equals."

I'm amused that she thinks she could ever be equal to a man such as myself who exudes power and strength. But something tells me she believes it with every shred of her being. I'll indulge the girl.

"If you fuck me over," I threaten and take her clit between my teeth. "I will kill you. Make no bones about it."

She whimpers when I bite hard enough to make my threat understood. Then, I suckle away the sting until she's squirming and begging me for more. I ease a finger into her and am satisfied when her tight cunt grips it. She'll feel amazing wrapped around my fat cock. My past wives were all used up whores. Their cunts had been nothing more than a wet hole to fuck. This cunt, though…it's a wet dream. A motherfucking fantasy come true.

"I won't fuck you over," she vows. "Please…I need…"

I take my time fingering her, making sure to locate her G-spot within. A tiny nub inside her that seems to beg to be touched. As I massage the pleasure spot, I tease her throbbing clit with the tip of my tongue. She squirms and wiggles and at times yanks on my hair. But it isn't until I suck hard on it that she comes with a scream. Her pussy clamps down around my finger as she shudders in ecstasy. I fuck her with my finger until she's ridden the orgasm into a relaxed state.

"Tonight, we seal the deal. All of it. You'll become Mrs. Diego Gomez. We'll get Buenaventura moving product again with your help. Together, we'll nail down the uncertain territories and make sure it is understood that we are bound. Everyone will know. Even Esteban and Oscar Rojas. There won't be a goddamned thing they can do about it." I grin at her as I make a dirty show of sucking her juices off my finger. "And I want you to wear this pretty white dress."

She sits up and attempts to right her dress. "I still want them dead. Knowing I've betrayed them won't be good enough. *I* want to kill them."

Sweet girl doesn't have it in her to kill anyone, but she has herself convinced. Who am I to crush her dark dreams?

"You'll get your chance," I vow. I give her a wolfish grin. "Aren't you afraid of marrying me? You have no idea what kind of man I am." When she narrows her eyes at me in annoyance rather than acting fearful, I stifle a laugh. "I hope you like anal."

"Ugh," she groans. "Don't be gross."

Finally, a motherfucking normal reaction.

"Mi diablita," I growl as I stand between her still slightly spread legs that are hanging off the desk. "There is nothing gross about my ten-inch cock buried deep inside your sweet ass. I bet you'll love it. You seem like the type of girl who has all sorts of sexual secrets. I'll discover them all."

She sobers up and presses her lips into a firm line. "I don't have secrets. What you see is what you get."

I grab her ass and pull her against my hard cock. I'm

dying to unzip my pants and shove my cock into her. But now that we'll be married soon, I'll wait for the sole act of consummating our marriage later.

"I know you're a very sexual person, Vienna," I murmur as I brush a soft kiss to her lips. "Every time I'm near you, your body responds. You want to be touched and pleased. You, my dear girl, have secrets you don't even know you have. You're about to hand over the key, and I will unlock every single one of them."

"Don't fuck me over, Diego," she threatens, her eyes hard.

I grip her jaw and kiss her brutally.

"You'll be mine soon. And nobody fucks over my wife," I growl as I nip at her lip. "Not even me."

IX | Vee

IT ISN'T UNTIL I'M BACK IN MY ROOM THAT MY MIND BEGINS to clear. What have I just done? I sold my soul to the devil, that's what. But what choice do I have? If I leave Diego, even if he does manage to rid this world of Esteban and Oscar, I can't possibly keep up my father's business without him. My only option would be to seek out other cartels. And I'd much rather deal with the evils I know, thank you very much.

I pace around the room as my blood pressure rises. What if this is an awful mistake? The man is smooth. What if he's simply biding his time until he gets what he wants? Will he kill me at that point? I'd gotten lost in his promises and expert touches. Let him seduce me so easily. *You'll be mine soon.* So possessive. His true feelings are every bit the same as Esteban's. I'm a thing to him—a power play. There never will be a legitimate partnership. As I left his office without my panties and my dignity dripping from me quicker than my arousal, I was reminded that it will always be me against them. I refuse to be owned by anyone ever again.

With a roar of frustration, I yank off the dress and toss it to the floor. I'm about to storm into the bathroom to take a cold shower when the door flings open. I sense his presence before I even see him. And I hate that a little piece of my heart patters that he came after me.

Sick girl.

Sick, sick girl.

Villain bait is what I am.

"Leave!" I snap and turn to point a finger at him.

His black hair is messy and it gives him a boyish quality. But the way he prowls toward me is far from boyish. I yelp when he grabs my hips and walks me back toward the bed. My fists beat on his solid chest through his vest.

"We're not done talking," he growls as he shoves me to the bed. "You were making deals one minute while letting me eat that perfect pussy. The next minute you're stalking off and slamming doors."

Before I can roll away from him, he smashes me with his muscular body. He snatches my wrists and holds them above my head with one hand. His mouth presses sweet kisses on my face, which only pisses me off. The motherfucker knows how to seduce me. Well, unlucky for him, my brain has over-ruled my pussy and—*oh God*!

He's managed to wiggle his way between my thighs and grinds his erection against me. His clothes are a thin barrier between us, so I feel every ridge of his cock against my body.

"You're mine," he starts again, his mouth stealing anoth-er kiss.

I turn my head to the side and scream. "I am nobody's!"

My rage rushes from me the moment he tickles me. I'm

pinned beneath him and have nowhere to go this time. Loud bellowing laughter escapes me as tears stream down my face. His fingers stop tickling me and he cups my bare tit. So many emotions are flooding through me that I'm getting dazed.

"Fine," he teases against my neck, the hot breath tickling me. "I'm *yours* then, fiancée."

He's clearly amused by my outburst because he chuckles. My hands are released as he starts kissing his way down between my breasts toward my stomach. I let out a gasp when he bites me near my belly button.

"I'm going to marry you in a few hours and then I'm going to fuck you so hard you won't be able to walk normally for days. Tell me no, mi diablita." His light brown eyes glimmer with feral hunger. I don't tell him no because villains are my kryptonite.

After having sex all the time with Esteban, my body seems to be going through withdrawals. All I can think about is how much I want this man's cock inside of me.

"Tell me you want to play big games with a big boy," he breathes as he trails kisses back up to my bare breast, making my nipple harden. His hand cups me between my thighs as he sucks on my nipple. And just like earlier, my body is eager for his touch. He massages me in that expert way that leaves me writhing in need for him. Diego turns my world upside down.

Another all-consuming orgasm is on the horizon. I need it because I want to feel alive and free again. To get lost in pure bliss even if only for a moment or two. The orgasm he gave me earlier was intense. With my mind crystal clear, as opposed to the months with Esteban that seem like a confusing fog, I'm able to feel every nerve ending as they all explode to life and sing at once.

"Say it, mi diablita," he growls, his fingers moving faster. "I'll do this all night until you say yes if I have to."

His words tip me over the edge and my orgasm tears through me with the force of a vicious tornado. I shudder from the sheer strength of it. Are all orgasms with him this intense?

He pinches my clit and I yelp. "Say it."

"I don't play games unless I know I can win."

His black eyebrow quirks up in amusement. "It's a good thing we're about to be on the same team then, huh? Because I *always* win."

I should feel threatened by this man but I'm not. Instead, I'm calculating a future. A future where I continue on with my father's legacy and nobody fucks with me ever again. With Diego, I can make this happen. He's a necessary move on the game board.

And if he tries to fuck with me?

I'll end him.

I don't know how, but I will end him.

"Say yes," he implores. His mouth finds mine and he kisses me, like a lover would. When he's touching and kissing me, it's easy to forget who we are and simply give in to the sensations. I could almost close my eyes and pretend we're something we aren't. That this is more than a business transaction. "Say it." He sucks on my bottom lip before popping off and staring at me with those beautiful pale brown eyes of his.

"Yes." I grit out the word and attempt to glare at him. My anger melts away when his mouth presses back against mine. The woman inside of me who is desperate for love and touch and intimacy falls victim to this expert-level game he's playing. She's down to spread her legs and hopes for the best.

The wounded soul within, though, is weary and suspicious.

"Vienna," he utters and gives me a serious stare. "I can kill a man without breaking a sweat. But women…"

I bite on my lip waiting for him to continue. His gaze falls to my mouth and he gives a slight shake to his head.

"That," he says as he runs his thumb along my lip and tugs it loose. "That is what has me making stupid decisions. *You* make me weak. You think I'm going to pull some bullshit to trick you, but you have no idea how vulnerable you make me."

My suspicion fades some and I give him a genuine smile. "I guess we're even then. Villains are *my* weakness."

Marriage.

A business arrangement.

A new last name and the key to a fortune.

My future.

"Dinner is ready. Diego is waiting," Tatiana says from my doorway.

"I'll be right down," I assure her with a smile. She gives me a lingering, sad look before leaving.

I smooth out my long red locks with a shaky hand. Ever since he left me needy and wanting earlier today, I've had a hard time getting a handle on my emotions. At some points, I feel confident in my choice to marry a cartel king. It was always my plan for as long as I can remember. Just with a different cartel king.

Thoughts of Oscar fill my head. My heart still aches. Over and over throughout my life, he broke my heart. But most times, it was unintentional. Other times…. This last time, he did it on purpose.

I want to cry. My heart is tight in my chest, and I have to swallow down my emotion. But I don't cry. I've cried more times than I can count over Oscar since I was five. That day when I met him, he told me to chase him. I've been chasing him ever since.

This is the last chase.

The one where I make him pay for what he did to me. He's a monster—not the man I always thought he was.

And Esteban?

My core clenches but it's purely a physical response. For so many months, he made me rely on him for everything. He conditioned me to grow addicted to him. But now that I've been weaned off, I know he's a monster too.

This marriage will help me eradicate those monsters. I'm not the adoring and loving little girl who follows around assholes like a lost little puppy anymore. I am worthy and capable. I am powerful. I am Vienna soon-to-be Gomez. Queen of the Cartel.

"That's an evil-villain smile if I ever saw one. Sure you aren't a villain yourself, mi diablita?" The deep voice from the doorway steals my attention.

"I'm certainly no angel," I bite back.

He smirks and holds a hand out to me. "Come. We have important things to take care of."

I swallow and make my way over to him on shaky legs.

My nerves are going crazy. When I'm near, he takes my hand and tugs me close. He's recently showered, and I inhale his masculine scent.

"You shaved," I observe, ignoring the way my heart beats wildly whenever he touches me. His goatee has been trimmed neatly. With his black hair styled messily and him looking dapper as hell in his three-piece black suit, I can't help but have a swell of pride. I know it's silly and girly and completely misplaced. But I allow the sensation to flood through me.

He'll soon be my husband.

I hope he doesn't kill me.

"You," he says, his voice low and gravelly. "You are a god-damned vision."

I laugh and shake my head. "No wonder you had so many wives. You're really good at this wooing stuff."

He smirks as he strokes my hair. I like that he pets me like I'm a kitten he's always wanted but nobody ever gave him, until now. The way he touches me makes me feel wanted and revered.

Please don't fuck with me, Diego.

"When you're my wife, I will cut out the eyes of all those who even look at you," he hisses as his mouth drops to mine. His hot breath tickles me. "And I will cut off the fingers of anyone who dares put his hands on you."

I shiver. My psycho villain siren should be wailing, but instead it is silent. The only sound is my heart thumping loudly in my chest. His violent words turn me on. I rub my thighs together and dart my gaze to his hooded one. "You're so romantic," I tease, my voice breathless.

His fingers slide into my silky hair, and he grips it. He

tilts my head back so he can stare down at me. Light brown eyes flicker all over my face as he inspects me. Then, he leans forward and kisses my forehead.

"Let's go eat, Vienna."

My God, this man is a tease. I swear he gets off on bringing me to the brink of insanity just to back off and leave me hanging.

"Come," he growls when I don't immediately follow after him.

"I'd like to, but someone is too busy playing the gentleman," I grumble back.

He smirks at me as his palm finds the small of my back so he can guide me out of my room. His hand slides to my ass where he grips it to the point of pain. "A gentleman doesn't grope his future wife on the way to their wedding."

I cut my eyes to his and grin at him. "I'm swooning, mi motherfucker."

He snorts and swats my ass. "I forgot you're a smartass."

"That's something you can't ever forget around me," I chide.

When we enter the dining room, I gasp. A feast has been laid out on the long rectangular table. Fancy silver and china decorate the space and several candles light up the room.

"It's beautiful," I breathe.

I'm not sure how this marriage thing will go, but it's already surpassed my expectations. Diego pulls out a chair beside the head of the table and gestures for me to sit. I take my place, folding my hands in my lap. He disappears and then reappears with Tatiana and Jorge. Once they're seated, he takes his place at the head of the table. A young male server comes out to fill our glasses with red wine and then he exits without a word.

"Tonight, we celebrate the union of two families," Diego says as he lifts his glass, his light brown eyes flickering with something that I hope is excitement. He certainly doesn't seem as apprehensive as I do. "Vienna and I will wed this evening under the eyes of God. If my mother, God rest her soul, were here, I know she would approve of my decision." His handsome smile warms me. The devil was an angel once. "Not only will this marriage be binding in the eyes of God, but it will be binding by our country's laws as well. And mostly," he says, his voice dropping to a low growl, "it will be binding to me."

I dart my gaze over to Jorge and Tatiana. Neither one of them speaks, but Tatiana flashes me a supportive smile.

"I keep my promises, Vienna," Diego murmurs. "I hope you keep yours as well."

I swallow and nod. The fierceness he's displaying would indicate that he believes what he says to be true.

I just wish I could believe it as easily as he seems to.

"So a toast to my future wife, a partnership that will strengthen my newly acquired empire, and for a play that will deliver ultimate revenge to our mutual enemies." He winks at me and holds his glass to mine. I clink it before quickly chugging down the bitter red wine.

"To Mr. and Mrs. Gomez," I agree, my voice shaking. "A power couple."

He reaches over and takes my clammy hand. "Mi reina."

"You may kiss your bride."

I imagined this moment a thousand times, especially in my early teen years, but with a certain dark-eyed boy. A fancy beach wedding in California with my father walking me down the aisle. A big, frilly dress. A giant fancy cake. The whole nine yards. With Oscar. And for awhile there, while high off my ass in Esteban's bed, he'd taken place as the groom in my fantasies.

But reality is oh-so different.

Diego Renaldo Gomez and Vienna Martina Berkley are the star of this show.

I'm still so dazed and in shock over what just happened that *my husband's* kiss takes me completely by surprise. His kisses are always soft but demanding. This kiss, though, feels like a promise. I don't get to enjoy his tongue that still tastes of wine because he ends our kiss as quickly as it began.

"Come now, mujer."

He guides me out of the old church toward where his fancy black car awaits. I am still trying to make sense of what's happening and staring at the gold band that sits on my ring finger when I hear what sounds like a pop.

"JORGE!" Diego roars a moment before he shoves me face first into the dirt.

A shriek escapes me. My palms sting, and I'm sure my knees are now scraped all to shit. I start to rise but then I'm tackled.

Pop! Pop! Pop!

"Stay down," Diego hisses against my ear. His body heat is no longer enveloping me as he starts shooting at someone on the other side of the car. Everything is so loud. Even though it's night time, the moonlight is bright. Diego crouches at the back of the car near the trunk. I dart my eyes under the vehicle. to see where the shots are coming from. When someone starts charging for us, I yell, "Two 'o clock!"

Pop! Pop!

The figure crumples into the dirt before they reach the vehicle. Shooting ensues from someplace else. I army crawl under the car until I'm close enough to take the gun from the dead man's grip. The shooting stops but my ears are still ringing. Two men are grunting, and I recognize one of them as Diego. Another figure emerges from the tree line on the other side of the road and starts charging for us. I squint my eyes to focus before squeezing the trigger.

Pop!

The bullet tears through his knee and he crashes to the dirt. When he looks up, he makes eye contact with me under the car. His weapon aims for me but then his head explodes. I'm gaping in horror when someone grabs my ankle.

"Diego!" I scream at the top of my lungs.

My attacker yanks me roughly out from under the car. As soon as I'm out, I aim the gun at his head.

"Whoa," Jorge says. "Whoa, niña."

He reaches for me, but I scramble to my feet without his help.

"Get in the car," he hisses. "Tatiana!"

She runs from the church and throws her arms around me. Her words are shaking and in Spanish. I yank the car door open before urging the frantic woman inside.

"Where's Diego?" I demand.

Two strong arms envelop me from behind, causing me to scream. Out of instinct, I drive the barrel of my gun behind me into what I hope is at my attacker's face. Before thinking twice, I squeeze the trigger.

Click.

"Fuck," Diego hisses into my ear. "Fuck, mi diablita."

Once I realize it isn't one of the bad guys, I collapse in his arms. He all but drags me to the car and shoves me inside. Tatiana sobs loudly as the men climb into the front seat. I pull her to me so I can stroke her hair.

"Shhhh," I coo. "We made it. We're safe."

She clutches my dirty dress, her tears soaking through my front. I hold her in a state of shock as Jorge hauls ass through the streets. He and Diego snarl in hissed tones the entire way home.

Her head tilts up and she palms my cheek. "I am so sorry, Vee. I worried this would happen. A marriage to a cartel leader is a lifetime of death and destruction."

I glance up to find Diego watching me, his jaw clenched. He's brutal and handsome and fierce in this moment. My words answer her question but I want him to hear.

"I know exactly what I signed up for and I am not afraid."

X | Diego

"I'M FINE, TATIANA," I SNAP AND SWAT HER HAND AWAY. Her brown eyes are filled with tears. We've barely been safely home for five minutes and she's mothering the fuck out of me. "It's a scratch. Tend to Vienna."

Vienna's brilliant green eyes dart to mine and she shakes her head. "I'm fine too."

I glower at her. She's far from fine. Blood drips down her shins from her knees. Her once pretty white dress is dirty as fuck. The red mane she'd worked so hard to smooth out is messy and tangled. Compared to Tatiana, who is shaking like a leaf, Vienna stands there like a horror from a nightmare. Hate-filled eyes. Calm demeanor. Full, pouty lips pressed into a firm, pissed off line.

"Get cleaned up and rest," I tell my doctor and close friend. "You're shaken up. I'll take care of Vienna."

Tatiana nods before hugging us both. Then, she disappears from my office leaving me alone with my *wife*. Jorge is already rounding up my men and heavily securing the compound. Those motherfuckers attacked me on my wedding day. I'd hoped it was some other cartel wanting to take me out. But deep down I knew. These were Camilo's men. Esteban and Oscar have already begun their war.

They don't care about Vienna.

Those assholes shot at her.

She's a tool to get to me, nothing more.

Rage bubbles up inside of me at the thought of losing her. Our business union is of utmost importance, of course, but I *married* her, goddammit. She's mine to protect. They almost took her from me.

"Were they with the Rojas's?" she questions, her voice level and even. Christ, she scares me with how calm she is.

I give her a clipped nod before snagging my cutter from the drawer. I prep the cigar from the ashtray and then light it. When we got back, I gave Jorge explicit instructions of what I needed him to do. Now, it's a waiting game. We'll be protected here, but I want those motherfuckers hunted down and brought to me.

"Now we wait," I tell her as I exhale a plume of smoke.

She walks over to me and plucks the cigar from my fingers. This wife is unlike my other pretend ones. Despite their constant bitching and nagging, they still feared me. Vienna takes this partnership seriously, apparently, because now we share *everything*. Even my fucking cigars and coffee. Her swollen lips wrap around the fat cigar and she inhales the smoke, her wild green eyes on mine. Fire and vengeance storm within them. My sweet girl wants to make them pay. I yank the cigar from her fingers and snub it out in the ashtray.

With a growl, I grip her jaw and tilt her dirty face up so I can regard her. This woman would have shot me in the goddamned face today had she had any bullets left. She's not a princess at all. Hell, she even warned me.

Vienna is the motherfucking queen.

I kiss her pouty lips hard, my fingers never leaving her jaw. Her mouth opens to kiss me back. Sweet. So fucking sweet. She grabs the front of my jacket to hold on as she jumps into my arms, her legs wrapping around my waist. I hold her perfect ass as we kiss. With her pressed against my eager cock, I'm dying to officially make her mine.

"We still have business, mi diablita," I growl between kisses.

She bites my lip and hisses. "Later, mi motherfucker."

We kiss hard with her grinding against my cock, but I can't proceed without knowing she's mine in every sense of the word. Her fingers start plucking at the buttons under my tie. Our kiss is messy and dirty.

"The contract," I snarl against her lips.

"Not now," she bites back.

I storm over to my desk and jerk her away from me to deposit her on the surface. The little minx tears her soiled dress from her body before tossing it at me. She's a goddamned dream sitting on my desk, looking hot as fuck in nothing but a simple matching nude-colored bra and panty set.

She's distracting me. For the future of our relationship, both personal and business, the contract needs to be carried out.

With my heated gaze on hers, I slip out of my jacket and pull off my tie. The vest hits the floor next and then I finish unbuttoning my shirt. Once I'm naked from the waist up, I grab one of my sharpest blades from my desk drawer. I flick it open, my eyes on hers to gauge her reaction. The little devil licks her dirty lips. My cock jolts, and I almost declare we fuck instead.

Almost.

"I want this gone," I tell her, pointing the tip of my blade at her bra.

"So do I," she says with a wicked smile.

I hook my finger under the bottom of her bra between her ample tits and pull it from her body. She remains still as I saw through the fabric with my knife. The material gives and frees her gorgeous tits. She tosses it away before leaning back on her elbows and putting her feet on my desk. Her knees fall apart as she offers her barely covered cunt to me. My dick is about to rip through my slacks to get to her.

"Danger makes your pussy wet. You really are a villain," I muse as I run my finger along the wet spot on her panties. "Such a naughty girl."

She bites her fat bottom lip and nods. I hook my finger into the side of her panties just below her clit to pull the material toward me. This too, I saw through eagerly. Once she's fully naked, I take a moment to appreciate her body. Young. Tight. Supple. She'd probably still be a virgin if Esteban hadn't have taken that away from her. Despite her past with him, she's still inexperienced. I love that she trusts me to take her to new places sexually. Whatever he did with her won't compare to what I'm going to do. I'm going to awaken her beast. I'm going to feed it and fuck it. There won't be any taming her beast. If anything, I'm about to free it.

"The contract is of utmost importance," I growl. "Then we can get back to what we both want and need." I tap my blade on the flesh over her heart. "I need *you* to remember every day that we have a promise to each other. Fuck witnesses."

"Just tell me where to sign," she grumbles, her voice breathless with need. "I need you."

I grab her left hand and pull it until she's sitting up. My mouth presses a kiss to the pale, perfect flesh on the back of her hand. The wedding ring that belonged to my mother sits proudly on her ring finger. Possessiveness thunders through me at seeing it there. I've held on to that one important item, the one materialistic thing my mother owned, for so long. Nobody was ever worthy of wearing it. But Vienna is the new owner, and I swear to God, it looks perfect on her.

"Do you need alcohol?" I question. "I might hurt you."

Her green eyes narrow. "I existed in a fog for too long. I want to feel everything."

I challenge her with my gaze as I tease her smooth flesh on the back of her hand with the tip of my blade. "A contract forged in blood. Still want to feel that?"

She snorts. "I'm not afraid."

I poke her flesh with my knife and become fixated on the crimson that wells around the hole before it spills down the side of her hand. She remains still as if to wait out my next move before breathing.

"Relax," I murmur. "It will be over soon."

A choked sound escapes her as I begin carving her flesh. I'm careful not to go too deep, but I brand my wife with a large *D* on the back of her hand. I don't want her to forget who she made this deal with. Ever.

When I finish, I meet her fiery gaze. Something that looks like a mix between hate and lust swims in her teary eyes. The tears don't fall, but I brought them to the brink.

"Fuck," I growl, my knife clattering to the desk. "You're so beautiful."

I grip her jaw and kiss her hard. Her fingers work at my belt and then zipper. Soon, she has my aching cock in her grip.

"Diego," she hisses as she fists my length. "I need you."

A groan rumbles from me as I rid myself of the rest of my clothes. I grip her hips and yank her to the edge of the desk. My cock is long and fat. She's so small. I should use lube to fit inside her without pain on her part.

But I can't wait.

I need her now.

"This is going to hurt," I warn through clenched teeth.

She claws at my biceps with blood running down her arm and draws me closer. "So hurt me."

The tip of my cock pokes at her slippery opening. She's practically dripping for me. Quick and fast. Like pulling off a bandage.

I slide an arm around her middle and meet her heat-filled gaze. My mouth crushes against hers a second before I drive powerfully into her. Her scream is snuffed out by my kiss, but I know I've probably hurt her. I'm about to black out from pleasure. She's the tightest fucking woman I've ever been with, and I'm inside her without a condom. I've been fucking women since I was fourteen. Not once did I ever do it without protection.

But this woman is mine.

"Jesus, you're perfect," I hiss out as my hips thrust into her again. Her fingernails continue to claw at my biceps, but she kisses me frantically. We're dirty and messy and so fucking needy for each other. Husband and wife. King and queen.

Two avenging angels turned devils escaped from hell.

She wraps her arms around my neck and leans against me, her mouth still fused to mine. I lose my footing and fall on my ass with her in my arms and my cock still buried deep inside her. Those manic green eyes meet mine as she reaches behind her to the desk. My knife that still drips with her blood comes into view. She pushes her palm against my chest, urging me to lie back on the floor.

"We weren't finished with our contract," she hisses, her body slowly rocking against me. I reach forward and pinch her clit, which makes her already tight cunt strangle my cock.

"So finish it," I challenge as I offer her my hand.

She laughs. The sound of it is downright terrifying. "I have something better."

She wraps one hand around the hilt of the knife and she covers it with her other bloody one. She meets my nervous stare with a confident one of her own. "You don't have tattoos on your chest. How come? The rest of you is covered in tattoos."

Are we really fucking talking about this in the middle of the hottest, messiest, most psychotic sex I've ever had?

"I want those scars to remind me of my past," I grit out, my dick throbbing with the need to come.

Her green eyes gleam with decisiveness. Then, she starts at my right shoulder with the tip of the blade. The pain is sharp and intense. She slices slowly, almost as if to punish me, along my chest before stopping just below my naval. Blood runs down my ribs in its wake.

"Vienna," I warn when she lifts the blade again and pokes deep into the flesh opposite of where she started. "Not so deep."

She loosens her grip and drags the sharp tip down to meet the ending point of her last cut below my naval. *V is for vengeance.* The pain is intense, but the throbbing of my cock is worse. I swat the knife out of her hand and grab her throat. Her eyes are shining with pleasure when I pull her close to my mouth. She places her palms right over the cuts on my chest for leverage and begins riding my dick like it's her sole purpose in life. I squeeze her throat until her pale face turns a gorgeous shade of purple.

Our mouths meet for another needy kiss. My grip on her throat loosens the moment her full tits start sliding against my bloody chest. Fuck, this is intense.

"Partners," I growl as I lift my hips to thrust into her. "Lovers." Thrust. "Mine."

She cries out and her body seizes, like the other couple of times I've gotten her off. The moment her pussy clenches around me, I lose it. My cock explodes its release deep within her. It isn't until I've drained the last of it and her shaking has subsided, that I let go of her neck. She collapses against my stinging and bloody chest. I hug her to me and kiss her dirty hair. Not even an hour ago, we were in the middle of a gun battle. Now, we're in a whole new type of battle. This battle takes more skill and so much more is on the line.

"I'm not on birth control," she whispers.

I stroke her tangled hair. "I know."

"But…"

"In my country, family is everything."

She relaxes. "That was…"

"Intense? Hot? Sexy as hell?" I quip.

Her chest trembles as she laughs. "I was going to say fucked up."

My fingers thread into her hair, and I tilt her head up so I can see her pretty face. Those fiery green orbs have lulled into a sleepy state. I love the look on her. "Mi diablita, you haven't seen fucked up yet."

She smirks, which makes my softening cock jolt inside her. "Bring it on, big daddy."

The black coat she always wears is gone. This time, she wears all white. The one who haunts me isn't a demon. She's an angel. I'm stunned as she walks over to me. Her pale arm is outstretched. Blood drips from it. I want to fix her. To make it stop. She brushes her bloody fingertips along my chest and draws a letter against my flesh.

V is for vengeance.

The angel straddles my hips and cradles my face. Her scent—so sweet—envelops me. The hood of her white cloak keeps her hidden from me. But deep down, I know she's the one I am looking for.

"Diego..."

"Diego."

My dream mixes with reality, and I have a hard time shaking away the recurring dream. Lately, because I don't sleep as much, the dream comes more often. I'm always awoken with a sense of loss. In the darkness, though, I am anything but alone. Curled up beside me is my wife.

"Diego," she murmurs. "It was just a dream."

She slides out of bed and soon the bathroom light comes on. When she returns, she has a wet cloth. The bed dips as she climbs back in. At least I can see her now. She wipes away the sweat on my brow with a serene smile on her lips.

Is this what my mother would have wanted for me?

All those months I had one "wife" after another in my bed. I was looking for them to fill up a part of me that was empty. But the void always remained. Yet now…now I feel better than I ever have. Vienna in my bed feels right.

"Do you have nightmares often?" she questions as she runs the cloth along my neck. My chest feels tight with every deep breath I take. Last night, after we showered together, I took her down to where Tatiana keeps the medical supplies and I used the medical super glue to fuse our wounds shut.

"Fairly so. Mostly a recurring one. Tonight it was different," I tell her with a sigh.

"Better or worse?"

"Definitely better. I just wish I could see her."

Her brows scrunch together. "You can't see her?"

I frown. "My mother believed dreams were prophetic in a sense. If she were still alive, I'd ask her about them. They started when I was a teenager after…"

Her fingertips brush against the scars on my face. "After this?"

"I almost died. I think hovering between life and death opened my mind a little."

She discards the rag on the end table and then curls up against me. It feels too nice to have her here. "What happened?"

"Camilo."

She stiffens. "He hurts lots of people."

"Not anymore," I growl.

Her palm rubs along my uninjured flesh on my chest. "Not anymore."

"My mother was sick. I stole from him. All I wanted was to make enough money for her to get the medical treatment she needed," I whisper, my voice distant. "He tried to kill me."

"But you fought him off? You ran away?" she questions.

I shake my head and hug her to me. With her supple naked body pressed against mine, I am calm and relaxed. "Someone saved me."

"Big bad Daddy Diego needed saving," she says with a laugh. "Hard to believe."

I chuckle with her. "An angel saved me."

"You must not be all bad then, villain, if an angel saved you."

Sitting up, I give her a grin before sliding out of the bed. I make my way over to the closet to dig around in my chest that holds a few of my mother's things. It's all I have left of my past. I lift the lid and root around until I find what I'm looking for. When I approach the bed, she's lying with her bare back to me. The contrast of her crimson hair against my white pillows is a sight I'll never get tired of seeing.

"They say when I showed up at the hospital, I was clutching this," I tell her as I toss my only memory of my angel onto the bed in front of her. I climb in behind her and pull her back against my sore chest. Her fingers grip the stuffed cat and she draws it to her.

"The bloody boy."

I frown at the smiling cat who has dried blood still on his

fur. "I suppose he is a little bloody."

"No, not Mr. Snuffles," she whispers. "*You're* the bloody boy."

She rolls onto her back, her green eyes the softest I've ever seen them. Her beauty temporarily distracts me from her words which don't make much sense. I've seen many expressions on Vienna's face but never one so tender and sweet. It's then that I hope I knock her up right away because I know she'll give our future children the same look my mother always gave me. My heart nearly explodes with the prospect of such an idea.

"I couldn't see my angel," I continue, my mind lost to that day. "I just heard her sweet little voice. A child. A child saved me, Vienna." I press a kiss to her forehead. "If it weren't for her stopping him, I'd be dead."

A tear streaks down her temple. "It was never supposed to be *them*."

I frown as I brush a red strand of hair away from her face. "Who, mi diablita?"

"You," she murmurs, awe in her voice. "It was *always* supposed to be you." Her fingertips dance across my scarred face. "I fixed you."

I fixed you.

It reminds me of all those years ago.

"I fixed him. He's going to get all better now."

My entire body stills as I stare down at her in confusion. A small, fearless girl. I'd never been able to recall what she looked like but I always remembered the sweet voice.

"*You* saved me," I murmur.

My palm reverently strokes her cheek. So often I thought about my angel. So many times I looked for her to thank her.

The bold little girl who tried to scare off Camilo Rojas when he was dead set on slicing me to fucking bits for stealing from him.

I slide my palm to her breast and she lets out a gasp. I take advantage of her parted lips and kiss her. I'm dying to convey my thanks to her. Her voice and her gentle touches kept me hanging on as I bled out on the grass. My lips brush against hers softly at first, but then I lose control. She's sweet—unlike any other woman I've tasted—and I'm convinced it's because she's truly an angel. Her tongue is tentative, but I don't care. My tongue shows her the way. I kiss her in a way that tells a story. The kiss is reminiscent of a time when she, although small, held my delicate life in her hands. I was enraptured by my little angel and latched on to her voice that seemed to keep me away from the darkness pulling at me.

I nip at her bottom lip and suck it into my mouth before diving in for another deep kiss. We're both breathless and panting by the time I reluctantly pull away. But only because I want to look at her.

Her long fingers reach for my face again. With whispering touches that remind me of that fateful day, she brushes her fingertips along my scars. Her eyebrows scrunch together and the tip of her nose wrinkles. She's so fucking adorable I could scream. I'm flying high on this new revelation. An unknown sensation stirs in my chest, and I like it. I really fucking like it.

Her green eyes darken with emotion. Tears shimmer in her normally fierce eyes as she regards me. "I thought you died."

"You saved me."

Her eyes are darting all over me. "Those bandages…they

124

couldn't have…"

"You ran off Camilo before he could deliver his death blow. Then, you stayed with me while I hovered between life and death. I knew I would find you again," I murmur before devouring her mouth once more.

I climb on top of her and ease my cock into her perfect cunt. In and out, I drive into her slowly. My eyes take in every little freckle that I took for granted until now. We fuck at an unrushed pace. She can't seem to stop touching my face, and I can't stop staring at her gorgeous features.

She is my angel. My fucking destiny.

She's mine.

And there's no way around it.

XI | Vee

I'M IN A DREAM.

A dream that consists of lying in bed all day every day where my romantic villain ravishes me until I'm spent and exhausted. For two straight weeks, he's had his men doing the dirty work while he does me.

It's heaven.

But when we fuck, it's something straight out of a porn mag from hell. Diego is a freak. Apparently, so am I. I have the bruises to prove it.

"I have a gift for you," Diego murmurs, his face buried against my bare chest.

I smile as I run my fingers through his black hair. "I thought what you gave me after breakfast was my gift."

He chuckles. "Nah, I was just hungry for your cunt. This gift is different."

"Should I be afraid?" I question, a flutter of butterflies dancing in my stomach.

He lifts up on an elbow and regards me with a sexy grin.

His hair is wild and his facial hair has grown out some. I think he looks the hottest when he's messy and disheveled.

"You never have to be afraid with me." He leans forward and kisses my lips. "But get dressed. I can't put this off any longer or I'll have a five foot nothing tigress flying all the way out here to maul me."

I frown in confusion. What the hell is he talking about?

"Get dressed, mi diablita."

Fifteen minutes later, I'm dressed in a jade-colored sun dress and have my hair pulled into a sleek ponytail. I'm sitting on Diego's lap in front of a laptop staring at the open Skype app.

"What are we doing?" I demand as I absently rub my finger over the big D on my hand. I'm still attempting to pick glue scabs off of it. His chest looks worse, though. Tatiana had a fit when she found out what we did and dosed us both up with antibiotics.

"We're making good on a promise."

"Okaaaaay," I huff. "I thought we were partners."

He bites the back of my bicep. "Remember that when she's yelling at me."

"Who—"

A beeping sound resounds from the computer. Diego leans forward to accept the call. Then, I'm staring straight into the big brown eyes of Brie. The sight of her has my chest squeezing and tears welling in my eyes. Last time I saw her, she was desperately trying to hold her husband's neck together.

"Vee!" she shrieks and leans forward to touch the screen. "Has he hurt you? He promised not to!"

I look over my shoulder at Diego and he gives me a

smug grin.

"Wait? Are you sitting in his lap? Oh my God," she growls. "Is he forcing you? I'm sending Daddy and—"

I snap my gaze to hers and snarl my words. "Do not send that man anywhere near me."

Confusion mars her features but then it sinks in. Her father killed my father. My father killed her husband.

"I'm sorry!" We both blurt out at the same time. Brie blubbers about how it isn't my fault. None of it is either of our faults. I'm barely keeping it together because she's bawling her eyes out. Diego hugs my middle and kisses my back, which calms me considerably.

A rogue tear slips out and I lift my hand to swipe it away.

"What is that?" Brie chokes out. "YOU BRANDED MY FRIEND?!" That comment was for Diego.

"What I did to him is far worse," I assure her with a teary laugh. "How are you? How's the baby?"

She stands and shows me her gigantic stomach. My friend is an adorable pregnant woman. "Two babies."

"Oh my God!" I squeal and touch the screen. God, I miss her so much.

"We're naming them Alejandra and Duvan," she tells me with pride. Sadness flickers in her eyes but mostly she's happy. Actually, I haven't seen Brie this happy in a long time.

"We're?"

She gives me a shy smile but doesn't get to answer me because some muscular guy walks in to the room where she's at and stands behind her. He's tatted up and wears tons of scars.

"Hey, Little Mermaid," a familiar male voice rumbles. The man leans forward, and I realize it's Ren.

"Ren!" I cry out and laugh. "Oh, wow, you've been

working out. You two are together now?"

He nods and presses a kiss to the top of her head. They're both so happy, which makes me thrilled for them.

Brie grows serious and guilt crumples her features. "I tried so hard to find you. You vanished. I had everyone exhausting their resources to find you. Even Diego," she says, motioning to him behind me.

His palm splays over my thigh and he slides it up under my dress, causing me to shiver.

"Esteban had me holed away in a shipping container," I tell her so softly it comes out as a whisper. "He hurt me."

Brie starts to cry and Ren comforts her. My man's way of comforting me is slipping his finger inside my panties to tease my clit. I bite on my bottom lip to stifle a moan. With a shaky voice, I recant my entire tale up until the part where they left me on Diego's lawn.

"Ozzie?" Brie asks in disbelief. "But he…how could he…"

I shrug. "And then Diego took me in. We made a pact."

At this, Brie winces. "You made a deal with him? Oh, honey, his deals suck."

I take offense to her words. Diego has been nothing but good to me for the past few weeks. "We're business partners," I grit out.

His palm creeps around to my grip my breast through the front of my dress. "And…"

I cover his hand with mine before meeting her gaze. "And he's my husband."

Brie's eyes widen and her mouth hangs open. "Oh, Vee…" Then she hisses at Diego. "What have you done? I trusted you! You promised to take care of her!"

With a growl of fury, I snap the laptop closed, ending her

tirade against the only man who has my back.

"Calm down, mi diablita," he grumbles as he slips his entire hand into my panties. He pushes a finger inside me, causing me to groan in pleasure.

"She has no idea what we have," I snap, anger simmering in my veins. "What we have is strong. I don't feel as though I was victimized!"

He chuckles as he slowly finger-fucks me. "Gabriella worries about you."

I stand up abruptly and hate that it forces his hand out of me. With my hands on my hips, I turn around to glare at him. "How do you two know each other, anyway?"

He shrugs. "I bought Duvan's territory and factory from her. I've looked after her ever since."

Jealousy surges through me. "One of your *weaknesses*?"

All humor is wiped from his face as he also rises. Today he's dressed fairly casual in a pair of black slacks and white-button down shirt. He's rolled up the sleeves, revealing his toned, veiny and tattooed forearms. Quite frankly, he looks good enough to eat. My pussy clenches with need, but I'm upset with him. So help me, if they had sex…

"Get that look off your face right now," he warns, taking a step toward me.

"Did you fuck her?" I hiss, my voice quivering. "Did she get to you like she gets to every other male on this planet?"

He launches himself at me, twisting me around with lightning speed before bending me over his desk. I scream and wriggle as he shoves my dress up. My panties are all but torn from me. And then he drives into me hard from behind. His fingers grip my ponytail and he yanks my head around, so I can see him as he fucks me.

"You're my wife," he snarls, his hips thrusting brutally against me. "She's a friend."

His thick cock stretches and fills me to the brink. With every pound into me, he brings me closer to orgasm. Our bodies were made for one another. A perfect fit.

"I'm inside *you*," he tells me, his voice soft. "I'm with *you*."

A jolting orgasm rips through me, and I shudder hard against the desk. He manages to thrust a couple more times before he comes with a roar. His hot seed spurts deep inside me. I love the way his body possesses mine.

Brie was wrong.

Diego is the best thing that's ever happened to me.

"Feel better?" he teases as he releases my hair before pressing a kiss to the back of my head.

"Much," I admit with a sigh.

He chuckles and slips out of me. His hot cum runs down my thighs. "Now put your panties back on. I'm hungry."

It came to me.

A sinister thought.

When Diego started pulling out fixings for sandwiches, my mind seemed to crack wide open. I fucking hate sandwiches.

"No," I grit out as I snag the loaf of bread. I storm over to the trash can and toss it inside. "No sandwiches ever."

His eyes widen in surprise, but then he does that thing he does where he reads me with one simple stare. I always feel exposed and transparent around him. But never vulnerable.

"Can we get something hot and filling?"

Understanding dawns in his light brown eyes. "I'll have Ingrid prepare one of my mother's dishes."

I beam at him and launch myself into his arms. "Thank you."

He palms my ass and bites my neck. "So easy to please."

"Speaking of," I tell him as I lean back to look at him. "I need some things from you."

"Like my ten-inch cock in your ass? All you have to do is ask, mi diablita."

I snort. "Ten inches. Kind of bragging there a little bit, huh?"

His grin is wolfish. "It'll feel like ten inches buried in your tight ass."

I press a kiss to his handsome mouth. "You make me happy."

He searches my eyes but then strokes my cheek with his thumb. "You make me happy, too. My mother would have loved you."

"And my father would have liked you, too."

"Where are we taking this discussion?" he questions.

I bite on my bottom lip as anxiety spikes through me. The things I need from him aren't going to be easy to acquire. "In your office. I think we need Jorge and Tatiana, too."

"Witnesses?" he muses with an arched eyebrow. Sometimes it's easy to get lost staring at his handsome face. When he sleeps, I often watch him for hours in the early morning light.

"More like helpers."

His eyes narrow, and I can practically see the wheels

turning in his head. "I'm probably not going to like this."

I kiss him again. "You're going to hate it."

He closes his eyes and shakes his head. "Why do I sense a 'but' somewhere in there?"

"But," I say with a smile, "I know you'll give it to me."

A growl rumbles from his chest. "So confident, I see."

I reach down and stroke his dick through his slacks. "The king gives his queen what she wants."

"And if I don't?" he challenges, his cock hardening in my grip.

"You will."

"Humor me, Vienna."

I tug at his belt and then unfasten his pants. His pale brown eyes darken a few shades. The way to Diego's heart is through his dick. His very thick, very scary, very long dick. I drop to my knees in front of him and fist his length. He lets out a hiss when I lick the tip of him. I can taste myself from earlier, and I like it.

"Say yes, Daddy D," I beg, giving him the most seductive look I can muster.

He groans as he wraps his hand around my ponytail. "You can't strong arm me into getting what you want by sucking my cock—fuuuuuck!"

I take him deep in my mouth. His giant cock doesn't get far inside before he's hitting the back of my throat. I grip the base of him and relax my muscles. Slowly, I ease him into my throat. Esteban face fucked me so many times that I learned to relax my throat in order not to choke to death. With Diego, I want to pleasure him. I want him to see how good we can be together. He lets me set the pace, and I'm thankful. Diego is a generous lover. While at times he's rough in a delicious way, he's never cruel.

I start to gag and pull off of him for a moment to catch my breath. When I look up at him, he's regarding me with a hungry emotion-filled gaze. I love how he stares as though I'm some god giving him a special gift. I lick my lips before sliding back down his length. The grunts and groans coming from him are making my panties grow wet. Him being so turned on is a complete turn on for me.

"Mi reina," he murmurs. My queen.

I hasten my efforts and pull out every pleasurable trick I can come up with. It's when I give his heavy balls a massage as I deep throat him that he lets out a familiar tell that he's about to come. His heat rushes down my throat, but I don't gag. I suck and swallow until he's gripping the sides of my head and pulling me from him.

"Come here, mi ángel hermosa," he growls.

I stand and he attacks me. His cock is still hanging out and his pants are around his thighs but it doesn't stop him from mauling me with a passionate kiss. He darts his tongue into my mouth and fucks it like he does my pussy at times. Hard and unrelenting. I'm so caught up in the kiss that I don't realize that his hand is under my dress and in my panties until his finger is rubbing my clit.

"Oh, God," I moan against his lips. His fingers are magical. He knows exactly how to touch me so that I'm practically humming with pleasure within seconds. And he does this little thing—"Diego!" I cry out and claw at his shoulders when he pinches my clit with his thumb and finger. Every time he does that, I swear I nearly explode. His cock, despite just coming, is pressing hard against me. "I need you."

He lifts me by my ass, and I help him out by wrapping

my legs around his waist. His finger hooks into my soaked panties and he yanks them to the side. I whimper when he starts pushing the swollen head of his cock into me. Each time he stretches me to the brink of pain, but it feels so good, too. I feel complete. Like he's the missing part of me. Once he's seated inside of me, his free hand is back in my panties searching out my clit. He always assaults my nerve-endings from every direction so that I'm on fire with pleasure.

"Bounce on my cock, mi diablita. Own what belongs to you," he hisses against my mouth. He pinches my clit again, and it makes me clench around him. I'm being impaled by a cartel king and I've never been happier in my life.

I grip his neck and use my feet, digging into his ass as leverage to work myself up and down over his length. All it takes is another pinch before I'm seeing stars. I shudder so hard, he nearly drops me. Then, my ass hits the cold counter top when he sits me on the edge. He's tall enough that he never has to break stride and thrusts hard into me from our new position. I rip at his hair as I seek his mouth. The moment our lips touch and tongues collide, he lets out a groan that's so animalistic, it speaks to my own inner beast. I want him to mark me from the inside out. And he does. Hot delicious come spills deep inside of me.

"Mine," he hisses against my mouth. "Vienna Gomez."

I tremble at hearing my name. I love it. The name sounds powerful. The name is powerful. But mostly, I love it because it's his name too.

"What were we talking about again?" he jokes as he slides his thick cock from my throbbing body.

"How you love me and are going to give me what I want," I tease back, a smile spreading across my face.

His eyes regard me, mixed with awe and some other strong emotion. I'd said he loved me in jest, but one look in his expressive eyes and I know. This is more than a business deal for him. Diego's feelings for me are real.

And this is exactly why he's going to give me what I want.

XII | Diego

ONIGHT, ON OUR ONE-MONTH WEDDING ANNIVERSARY, we are celebrating with an enormous party. The wealthiest people from all over Colombia have been invited. Security has been tripled, but I still don't feel safe.

Give me what I want, Diego.

I grit my teeth. You'd think with five wives prior, I'd have plenty of practice telling a woman no. Instead, I fall into my wife's dick-sucking traps and hand her the keys to my kingdom without hesitation. She asks and I give. Every single time. I even had to call in the favor Gabriella owed me. Boy, was she upset, but she delivered.

I hold up the jewelry box—which arrived today, just in time—and lift the lid. Gabriella had to scramble to get me these earrings, but I wanted them for tonight's celebration. Perfect timing. Everything is going too smoothly, which has my chest tight with nerves.

"I don't like this," Tatiana tells me with a huff. Her gaze is on my bare chest and she fixates on one spot.

"I promised her," I snap as I start buttoning my shirt back up. "Vienna gets what she wants."

She frowns and crosses her arms over her chest. Tonight she's donning a black sequined gown for the fancy affair. "I don't like when her wants affect you."

I shrug as I knot my tie. "It doesn't matter what you like. This is bigger than how you feel, Tatiana."

"I just…" she trails off with tears in her eyes. "Would your mother want you risking it all on some woman?"

I pin her with a serious stare. "My mother would have wanted me to risk everything for love."

She swallows and her bottom lip trembles. "So this is love?"

"It is for me."

"And for her?"

"Only time will tell." I shrug on my black vest before pulling on my black suit coat. "Everything will be okay."

Her head bows but she gives me a small nod. "I hope so, Diego. You're like a son to me. I can't lose you over some girl. You fell too hard and too fast for her. It scares me."

I scrub my scruffy cheek with my palm before giving her a tender smile. "Vienna and I have a past that has led us to this moment. Fate was always playing an intricate game with our lives. We've finally gotten here. I'm not going to disregard what was designed for us. It's been a long road getting here and the road still has some twists and turns. We'll get to the end, though, together. I trust her and she trusts me."

Tatiana rushes over to me and hugs me. "You always were weak for women."

I pat my close friend's back and kiss her on the top of her head. "This woman makes me stronger. She's tough and resilient. Exactly what someone of my position and caliber needs. An equal, Tatiana. I don't have to take care of Vienna because she takes care of us both."

"I hope you know what you're doing," she says finally.

I wink at her when she pulls away. "I don't and that's half the fun."

"That's him," Vienna says, her long manicured nail pointing at the security monitor. "He'll come for me."

"He won't leave with you," Jorge assures her. "We'll have eyes on him at all times."

She turns to regard me, and I study her face for insecurity, fear, any-fucking-thing, but I find nothing. Her chin is lifted and her green eyes are sharp. My sweet wife isn't afraid. If anything, she's thirsty.

"Are you sure you want to do this?" I question, my brows pinched together. "Do you still have the knife?"

She slides up her silky brilliant green evening gown, past her knee to reveal a garter belt with a knife tucked inside. It's hot as fuck and if I didn't have one of my enemies in my home at this very moment, I'd screw her against the closest wall.

"I can do this, Diego," she assures me with a bright grin, releasing her dress as she walks toward me. "*We* can do this."

Her gorgeous red hair has been twisted and pinned into a fancy style behind her head. A tendril has escaped on the side of her pretty face, and I can't help but tuck it behind her ear. She's beaming at me. Confident. Fierce. Strong as hell. Mine.

"You look beautiful, mi diablita," I tell her and press a soft kiss to her glossy lips.

She slides her palms up over my chest to my neck. "You look handsome, mi motherfucker."

Everything inside of me screams to pull her into my arms and never let go. She'd be safer that way. In the short run. But what about the long run? What about for the rest of our lives? I have to let her fly away from me for a bit because that's the only way to keep her.

"I have something for you," I tell her with a wolfish grin as I pull out the jewelry box from my pocket.

Her lips quirk up on one side. "You're such a romantic."

"These," I say as I open the box to show her the two shiny diamonds, "came all the way from America. Your friend Ren's dad acquired them for me. They're special. Like you."

She stands on her toes and gives me a chaste kiss. "Thank you, Diego. Thank you for this." Her past hurts and injustices are written all over her face. I can give her security. I can give her safety. I can give her me.

She puts both earrings in and grins at me. "How do I look?"

I grab her hips and tug her to me. "Good enough to eat."

"He's headed toward the stairwell, Mrs. Gomez," Jorge says from his chair in front of the monitors. "You should go."

My hands are locked on her waist. It takes every ounce of self-control to remove my hands and not crush her to me. "Be safe, Vienna."

Her palms find my cheeks, and she tugs me down for a kiss. "I'll be okay as long as you have my back."

Our kiss turns frantic, but then she's pulling away.

"I have to go," she whispers.

I grip her jaw and glare down at her. "I love you, mi diablita."

Tears glisten in her gorgeous green eyes. "I love you too."

The moment she's gone, I prowl over to the wall of monitors. Jorge has her in view because as soon as she leaves the room, she's on the screen. When we'd discussed this party a couple of weeks ago, I spared no expense outfitting one of the spare rooms with wall-to-wall monitors of every part of the house, both inside and out. The equipment picks up sound as well because I needed to be able to have eyes and ears on her.

We watch my enemy slip into her old bedroom. She's long since moved into my room. I love that she's begun to add touches to the home to make it hers. Despite her and Gabriella's conversation ending with Vienna hanging up on her best friend a couple of weeks ago, she's still stayed in touch with her friend Ren. He even went by her parent's house and had some of her belongings shipped here. This is her home now. With me.

"What's he doing?" Jorge asks.

"He's looking for the book with their pictures in it."

Sure enough, he walks over to the bookcase and pulls *The Count of Monte Cristo* from the shelf. He's thumbing through it when Vienna walks into the room.

"Turn up the sound," I bark out.

Jorge turns the knob just as Vienna says in a choked voice, "Oscar?"

Over the past month, my wife has shared with me more and more stories of her past. A lot of them revolved around this man. Someone she trusted. Even loved. A man who should have protected her. Instead, he took from her and used her.

"Vee," Oscar replies as he shoves the book back into place and then turns to regard her. From my vantage point, I don't see any weapons. "You look well." His tone is flat and cold. It makes my hackles rise.

"I'm a good actress. I'm doing what I can to survive," she tells him, her voice shaky.

He takes a step forward, but my brave woman doesn't retreat. She lifts her chin to meet his gaze dead on.

"You were supposed to kill him," he bites out.

She stiffens. "And I told you, I'm not a killer. I'm scared."

His answering scoff is brief, but I catch it. "Kill him. Tonight. We'll be waiting for you to carry it out." He approaches her, and I hate how close he is to her. "Where'd we go wrong?" His hand lifts and he runs his finger along her jaw. She shivers as if she's waited for that touch her entire life. But I know my girl and I know when *I* touch her like that, it's different. Her reaction to me is so much better because it's real.

"You hurt me," she accuses, her bottom lip wobbling. "You *both* hurt me."

He runs his fingers through his long hair that touches his shoulders. "It was just because it was a part of the plan. None of it meant anything. You know that. A big game of fucking pretend, Vee."

I keep waiting for her to lash out, but she remains calm. She sniffles and he reaches to swipe away the tear. Instead of flinching, she leans into his touch.

Good girl.

"I'm sorry," he says, his voice raw. And I hear it. Remorse. Regret. But it doesn't forgive what he did to her. She'll never get over that.

142

"Oscar…"

"Does he hurt you?"

She looks away, as if to not meet his gaze, but her eye is on the hidden camera. "Yes." Her green eyes flicker with deception before she darts them back to him. "Every night in this bed. He takes and takes and takes. I was forced to become his wife." Her shoulders hunch as she starts to cry.

Fake. Fake. Fake.

My queen doesn't cry.

"Oh, Vee," Oscar croaks as he hugs her to him. "It was supposed to be us. How'd we get so lost along the way?"

I slam my fist on the table and hiss at Jorge. "Lost? He fucking ignored her their entire lives. Dragged her around like she was his fucking puppy. And then he raped her for authenticity?! This kid is fucking quacked out."

Jorge grunts in agreement.

"Can you get me out of here?" she pleads. "We can run away. Esteban doesn't have to know." Exactly what he wants. His sweet, adoring girl worshipping him at his feet.

He squares his shoulders and cups her cheeks so he can look at her. "We still need you to kill Diego. He'll always be a threat to us. Once he's gone, we can move on together."

"Esteban…" she murmurs.

He lets out a possessive growl. "We'll deal with Esteban later. He's unhinged, Vee. Together we'll take care of him. Then it will just be us." His mouth drops to hers where he places a soft kiss on her lips. Rage threatens to consume me, but Jorge is gripping my shoulder tight.

"Relax."

I crack my neck and clench my jaw. "I'll relax when that fucker is dead."

Vee pulls away from their kiss and darts her gaze to the camera again. She's playing the part of fearful girl, but I see the fire in her eyes. With one simple look, she assures me she knows exactly what she's doing. I have to trust her.

"How?"

He walks over to the bed, pulls a knife from his belt, and lies down. Then, he motions for her. "I'll show you."

She takes his hand as she climbs onto the bed with him. He urges her to straddle his waist. It takes some maneuvering in her fancy dress but she sits on him, her garter belt barely covered by the fabric. If he finds her knife, that could be a problem. I rise from my chair to ready myself to intervene if necessary.

"Use this knife," he instructs. "Put it under your pillow like this." He shoves his knife under the pillow. "Now, when you're fucking, lean in to kiss him but pull the knife out. Then, stab him. So easy, Vee. You can do this." His palm slides up her thigh.

"Wait," she blurts out and threads his fingers with hers before he notices her knife. "He's usually the one on top. What then?"

He smiles and flips her onto her back. His mouth finds hers as he kisses her hard. The motherfucker's hips are moving as he grinds against my wife's cunt.

Trust in Vienna.

Don't fuck this up by being a hothead.

"Mmm," she moans out in pleasure. But it's fake. When my sweet woman moans, it doesn't sound like that. Her moans are more ragged, more breathy, less controlled.

"If I had more time, I'd make love to you right here in this bed, Vee," he coos. "Just like I should have done all those years ago. It was supposed to be us. I've made so many mistakes."

"Rape is more than just a mistake, fucker," I snarl at the screen.

"But," he continues, "we can get past those. I wasn't in my right mind then. From here on out, I'll show you how good we can be together."

"Okay," she agrees. "Just us. Now show me how to kill Diego."

He holds her wrist with the knife in it and brings it to his chest. It would be so easy for her to kill him but that isn't part of the plan. At least not yet.

"You can do this, baby," he tells her and kisses her sweet mouth. He grinds against her again. "God, I wish we had more time."

"Soon," she promises.

When he pulls away, her dress reveals her hidden knife. She discreetly covers herself when he gets distracted by cupping her tit.

"Tonight," he reminds her in a gruff voice. "End this tonight and you can come home. We'll finish it together. Just you and me, baby."

She sits up and smiles at him. False and transparent. But only to someone who sees her genuine smiles each day. "You'll be waiting for me?"

"Just outside of the compound. If you're not out by morning, we'll know something went wrong. I'll come back for you if that's the case," he assures her.

Such a fucking hero.

She slides off the bed and launches herself into his arms. "I've missed you."

"I know you have," he agrees as he strokes her hair. "I have to go."

Her hand slides to his front and she gives him one of those sexy as fuck pleading looks she gives me sometimes. I'm unable to tell her no. The girl always gets what she wants. And this chump isn't immune.

"This isn't fair, baby," he groans. "You know we can't fuck right now and yet you're going to send me out of here with blue balls."

She pouts but releases his cock. "Fine."

He laughs and gives her a smug grin. "Soon, baby. I promise." He shoves a small piece of paper into her palm. "If shit gets too hard, this is how you can reach me."

Their mouths meet in a heated kiss and then he tears himself from her. He slips out of the room and down the hallway.

"Keep an eye on him," I growl at Jorge as I watch Vienna.

She walks into the bathroom and proceeds to immediately brush her teeth. I wish there were time to haul her into the shower with me to wash that man's stink off her, but there's not. We have a party to attend.

"He's at the tree line," Jorge tells me. "A car is waiting."

"Are there any others here? Any of his men?"

"Not as far as I can tell."

"Good."

I stalk from the room on a mission to find my wife. Once I'm in her old room, she throws herself into my arms.

"Oh, Diego," she murmurs, her voice quaking. "Why is this so hard?"

I kiss her neck. "It'll get harder before it gets easier. You did great, mi diablita."

She pulls away to regard me with guilt in her eyes. I hate that she feels guilty for what we both know had to be done. "It's hard to turn off love for someone. Even when you move on. Even when you hate that person."

I kiss her soft lips. "I know. It will all be over soon."

"Come here," I growl as I tug her to me in the hallway. I sway on my feet because my sweet wife has taken it upon herself to get me plastered at our celebration. She, on the other hand, is quiet and contemplative. She'd nursed the same glass of wine all night.

"No," she teases.

This girl loves it when I chase her down and fuck her into the next day.

"Now," I order.

"No!" she screeches as she bolts down the hallway.

I'm uncoordinated as I run after her, shedding my coat along the way. I see a flash of red hair dart into her old bedroom, so I charge after her. Once inside the room, I rip off my vest and begin working on my tie.

"Get naked," I bark, meeting her gaze with a heated one of my own.

"No," she challenges. "Leave me alone."

I smirk as I jerk the tie away from me. "I'll never leave you alone. In case you've forgotten, you bear my mark. Now take off your goddamned dress before I cut it off you."

She screams and backs herself into a wall. I stalk for her as I tear through the buttons on my shirt. When I'm near, she goes to dart past me, but I'm able to easily snag her into my arms. She wiggles in my grip, but I manage to rip the zipper down her back. My wife fights the entire time as I pull off her dress. The garter belt remains but the knife has long since been put someplace else.

"Get away from me," she hisses, her green eyes flaring with fury.

"Fucking never," I snarl back at her. "Take off your panties."

"No."

"Goddammit, woman!"

It takes some wrestling, but I manage to pull off her undergarments as well. I toss her onto the bed and drop my pants in the next instant. She starts to crawl away, but I snag her thigh in my brutal grip.

"Ahhh!" she cries out when I drag her back to me.

I pin her wrists at her hips. She wriggles but doesn't fight me when I start kissing the inside of her thigh toward her pussy.

"Stop," she breathes. "Don't do this."

Her cunt begs me to, though. It drips with her arousal. I run my tongue along her seam and lap up her sweet taste. She shudders in my grip.

"You're mine," I growl and tug at one of her pussy lips with my teeth.

"Never," she lies.

I suck on her clit until she starts convulsing with pleasure. Before she can recover, I climb over her body and press the tip of my cock against her wet opening. Her body accepts me despite her clawing on my shoulder and screams. Our eyes meet and an emotion I love dances in her eyes.

"I love you," I murmur softly against her lips.

She starts to cry, and I fucking hate it because it sounds so real. My fierce Vienna doesn't cry. "Please," she sobs. "I can't do this."

I nip at her lip. "Yes you can. *We're* doing this."

As I thrust into her, I lift up so I can watch my dick slide into her wet cunt. Her fingertip runs along my chest and she makes a cross motion.

"X marks the spot," she says sadly. Then, her hand disappears under the pillow. Everything happens so quickly. One minute I'm fucking my wife and the next, she's plunging a shiny knife into my chest.

"Mi diablita," I hiss in shock.

"I am not yours," she chokes out as she shoves me off of her.

I roll onto my back and stare down at the knife that sticks out of my chest. Her green eyes are fixated on the wound that now gushes with blood. She's frozen in horror, and I'm in too much pain to move.

"Diego—"

I hiss the nastiest words I can muster. "So help me, cunt, you're going to die for this."

She snaps out of her daze and throws on a T-shirt and a pair of jeans. I clutch my chest but don't dare remove the knife.

"Vienna," I croak out. My eyelids grow heavy. Last time I got stabbed this deep, I nearly died on the lawn on the side of this very house. Back then, it was a demon who tried to kill me. This time, it's mi ángel.

The door clicks shut and I know she's gone.

The pain in my chest is from something altogether

different than the knife stuck in my flesh.

Loss.

Heartache.

A crack in my soul.

Blackness floods in around me. I hear voices, two in particular, but I tune them out so I can chase the vision in my nightmares. She'd abandoned me when I'd married Vienna. But now she's back. My ángel wears all white, but her gown drips with blood as she beckons for me to follow her.

I know wherever she wants me to go is going to hurt.

But I'd follow her anywhere.

"Diego!"

The voices call to me, but I don't like them. The soft whisper of my angel is sweeter. It's more alluring. It drags me away from all of this.

I'm coming, ángel …

Black.

Black.

Black.

PART THREE:

"Uprising" by Muse

XIII | Vee

RUN.

Run.

Run.

Tears stream down my face as I bolt out the front door barefoot and down the gravel drive. Rocks bite into my flesh as I run as fast as my legs can carry me.

They wanted me to kill him.

And they got what they wanted.

What about what I want?

I sob and swipe at my tears to clear my vision. It doesn't matter what I want. If I got what I wanted, I wouldn't be soaked in my husband's blood and running without a backward glance. My ankle rolls, and I nearly stumble face first into the rocks but I quickly recover.

Don't look back.

Don't look back.

I do look back, though. The house, giant and imposing—a castle to a fire-breathing dragon queen—mocks me. It practically hisses its hate at me. I'm a traitor.

Pop!

The sound of a gun behind me scares the shit out of me. It wouldn't be the first gunfight I've been in, but I don't have Diego and Jorge trying to protect me this time. This fight has Jorge firing *at* me rather than *with* me.

Pop! Pop!

The gravel near my feet kicks up as a bullet ricochets. I scream and run harder. The property is huge and it feels like the run down the driveway is the longest mile I've ever run. My lungs are seized up in pain and my calves scream from exertion.

Don't stop.

If you stop, you'll lose.

If you stop, everything you worked so hard for will be gone in a poof of smoke.

"Get back here, you bitch!" Jorge bellows from behind me. He's getting closer because now I can hear his grunts as he runs. With him wearing shoes, he'll catch up to me soon.

The sound of a car engine blares to life and then a car squeals from its spot on the road ahead, heading right for me. I wave my hand, hoping it's Oscar. The last thing I need is to run right into the arms of yet another monster. The monsters I know are the ones I'll keep.

"Stop!" Jorge roars from behind me as he gains speed.

The car slows to a stop at the end of the driveway and the passenger door gets flung open. Just like he promised, Oscar waits behind the wheel. A bullet whizzes past me and pings the metal of the car.

So close.

A few more feet.

I dive into the seat and Oscar wastes no time peeling away even before I manage to close the door. When I turn to look at him, he's grinning. His palm slides over my shirt and he cups my breast. Diego's blood has soaked through my clothes.

"You did it, baby," he says, pride in his voice. "We're getting you the fuck out of here."

I start to cry and he pulls me as close as he can to him with the console between us. My heart is hammering in my chest and the sense of loss is crushing.

I can't do this.

But I already am.

Of all the villains in my life, Oscar is the easiest to handle. I've known him since I was five. I can interpret his every expression. Every lie he tells, I can sense. For these reasons, he'll be both the hardest and the easiest man to beat. I'll know how to hurt him but in turn it'll hurt me because of the past we shared.

"Where are we going?" I question as the trees whiz by in the darkness.

His hand settles on my thigh and he squeezes. "Buenaventura."

"I thought Diego took over there."

He grins at me. "Diego has been distracted. I think he took on more than he can handle. Esteban and I rounded up some men. We were easily able to take it back over. Some of the men turned on him to spare their lives and fed Diego false information. Others, we've needed to torture to get what we want. But it's ours and it's only the beginning."

I frown as I frantically try to figure out what this means for me. I'd expected to encounter Oscar and Esteban. Not an entire branch of the cartel. I'm about to ask more questions when Oscar's phone rings.

"Yeah?"

I can't hear what he's saying but I recognize Esteban's deep voice on the other end.

"I have her. It's done." Oscar pauses to give me a chaste kiss. "We should be there by breakfast."

They hang up and he lets out a sigh. "We can't let him know about us at first."

I refrain from rolling my eyes. There will never be an "us," buddy. "Okay," I breathe and then let fear filter into my voice. The fear is real. With Esteban, there's no faking the emotion. "I'm scared he's going to hurt me. I don't want him to drug me again."

Oscar lets out a growl. "I'll do my best to not let that happen."

We drive several hours through the night without stopping. Eventually, Oscar pulls off onto a side road. Dawn has breached the horizon, but it's still fairly dark out due to a storm that's rolling in.

"I have to take a piss," he tells me as he climbs out.

I get out as well. My fingers go to my earrings and I rub them. They're so beautiful and important. The ring Diego gave me no longer resides on my finger, which makes my chest ache. It is sitting on the end table in the room he and I shared. Safe. Unlike me.

Breathe.

You've got this.

You knew it would be hard.

I'm jolted from my thoughts when Oscar hugs me from behind. A chill races down my spine as he gropes my breasts.

"All these years and we're just now getting together," he murmurs as he kisses my shoulder. "How stupid were we to wait this whole time?"

I let out a gasp when one of his palms slides to cup me between my legs. I know what needs to happen. What *will* happen. It just doesn't make it any easier.

"We better fuck now before we get there. Esteban is going to make things difficult for us until we carry out our plan," he tells me as he starts working to unfasten my jeans.

I grip his wrist to stop him. Distract him. Delay the inevitable. "What is our plan?"

He works my jeans down over my hips and rubs at my pussy. "We kill him."

"I know, but how," I demand, a little too harshly and out of character. I soften my words and lean against him as he massages me. "I want us to think of something before we get there."

His finger pushes into my dry opening, drawing a whimper from me. "I'll stab him in the back."

How appropriate…

"When?"

He works his finger in and out of me as if he's actually bringing me pleasure and not discomfort. "Next time he's balls deep inside you. That'll be when he least expects it."

"Maybe we should go then," I suggest, my teeth gritted in pain every time the edge of his fingernail scratches inside of me. "Get it out of the way."

"Soon," he assures me. "Your pussy is dry, baby."

I shudder. "It's been a long night."

He eases his finger out of me, and I let out a sigh of relief until he pushes me down over the hot hood of the car.

"Oscar," I start, disgust overwhelming me to the point I might throw up. "Maybe we should do this later." His belt jangles behind me, and I hear the tear of a foil. "Ozzy," I whimper. "Ozzy, why don't we—" Pain burns through me as he enters me dry from behind. Hot tears leak from the corners of my eyes as I clutch the hood. "Ahhh!"

"I know, baby," he coos as he thrusts into me hard and pets my hair. "Feels so good for me, too."

A sob catches in my throat, but I refuse to let it escape. My mind drifts to Diego.

"Mi diablita, these are bad men. They'll rape you," he hisses. Despite his horror-filled words, he's cupping my face in a gentle way that makes my heart flutter.

"It wouldn't be the first time," I clip out.

His expressive light brown eyes seem to flicker with his pain. "I don't know if I can allow this."

I lean forward and kiss his soft mouth. "It's the only way."

He rolls me over to my back on the bed and he starts pressing kisses all over my face. "I can't part with you."

I swallow, fighting stupid tears. "You can."

"What if they hurt you?"

"I'm stronger than you think."

He pushes his thick cock into my body, that is always wet for him, and makes love to me slow and sweet. Once he's come deep inside of me, his mouth finds my ear. "I want to trust in you, mi reina."

"You must," I whisper. "You absolutely must."

"Fuuuuck," Oscar groans, dragging me to the present. He pulls out and gives my ass a squeeze. I remain bent over the car as he ties off the condom and tosses it in the woods. "Plenty more of that in our future."

I pull myself up into a standing position and jerk my jeans back into place before hopping back in the front seat. He doesn't seem bothered at all by the fact that I was an unwilling participant. As he starts up the car, he fishes a couple of pills from his pocket. "Need something to take the edge off?"

"I told you, I don't want any drugs," I hiss.

He frowns and takes one. "I'm not going to hurt you. Not like him. I love you, Vee."

Too late, asshole.

All I want to do is curl up in a ball. But I need this guy with me…not against me. I lean against him and let my fatigue take over. He wraps an arm around me and strokes my hair as we drive. I want to stay awake but I'm too overcome with emotion.

I gladly run to Diego in my dreams.

"Like this," Diego tells me as he grips my wrist and guides the knife to his chest. "Plunge hard so it doesn't fall out. If it comes out, I'll bleed out."

I wince at his words. Hard. Got it. "Is this necessary?"

"You know how those motherfuckers are about their authenticity. They want authenticity, we'll give it to them."

"But…" I trail off, my throat squeezing with emotion. "What if it slips? What if Tatiana isn't right? What if we mess up?" I toss the knife onto the desk with a grumble.

His thumb drags along my jawline and he grins at me. Stupid fucker isn't scared of anything. Not even death. "If we mess up, I'll see you in hell, mi diablita."

I huff and roll my eyes before wriggling away from him. He grabs my hips and pushes me against the edge of his desk. His strong hands spread my knees apart, and he slides my dress up my thighs. A moan escapes me when he rubs my clit through my panties. He glares at me while he brings me pleasure. "I'm more worried about what happens to you afterward. What happens to me is nothing. What happens to you is everything."

I soften at his words and clutch his face. He kisses me hard as his finger rubs me between my legs. My panties are soaked with his assault, but I don't stop him. Pleasure with Diego comes so often that I've become greedy for it. Downright addicted.

"Just tell me no at any time and we'll find another way," he murmurs against my mouth. "I know this was your idea, but it's okay to change your mind."

An orgasm seizes me, and I shudder until my muscles feel as though they are jelly. When I come down from my high, I regard him sadly. "V is for vengeance. I want to make them pay and this way gets me right where I need to be."

He nips at my lip and grins. "So we give the girl what she wants. Anyone ever tell you you're spoiled?"

I laugh and tug his tie so he remains close. "You're the one who spoils me."

"And I'm about to spoil you with my mouth," he growls.

"Wake up," Oscar bellows.

I jolt upright and squint against the bright morning sun. We're parked in front of the shipyard. Shipping containers are stacked at least ten high for as far left and far right as the eye can see. Beyond the long strip of metal containers are the barges that ship cocaine, among other products, from Buenaventura to San Diego via the Pacific.

As a girl, we visited their shipyard often. But after my stay in one of the metal tombs for months back home in the States, I can't help but feel overly apprehensive about being near them again.

"Let's go," Oscar says as he climbs out.

I follow after him and squint against the sun. "I'm scared."

He gently grabs my elbow and leans into me. "There are eyes everywhere, baby. Just play it cool. I'm scared too, but we'll get through this."

I let him guide me across the gravel parking lot to the gate in the chain-link fence that stands wide open. A man with an assault rifle stands at the gate but nods at us to go on through. I shiver and try to stick close to Oscar.

"Where are we going?" I squeak out.

He points to the shipyard office. "Esteban wants to ask you some questions."

Terror climbs its way up through my throat at having to

see him once again. Not that long ago, he had such a strong hold on my life. That won't happen again. I'm not his for the taking. At least not permanently.

I belong to someone else.

My heart skitters in my chest. So many what-ifs scream at me from the back of my mind but I refuse to give thought to any of them. Those what-ifs will knock me off my game. I can't afford that distraction.

I'm still trying to push those thoughts away when the cold air from the office billows out around me as Oscar opens the door. It's dark inside. I'm shivering but it has nothing to do with the temperature. It has everything to do with the beast that lives and breathes inside. The snarling beast who I will soon make my prey.

"Roja."

XIV | Vee

ONE WORD.

One simple nickname.

Spoken with such promise.

I'm scared shitless.

"Esteban," I choke out.

Unlike Oscar would, he doesn't run up to me for an embrace. Instead, he emerges from the shadows like the Boogeyman. Tall. Imposing. Powerful. I suppress a whimper of fear. Everything about him seems bigger and fiercer. His neck is most definitely thicker and his dress shirt is stretched to the limits across his bulky chest. Esteban has turned into the Colombian Hulk.

He narrows his eyes at me before flicking his gaze over to his brother. The way he watches us worries me. Esteban is like some feral animal who can probably smell the stink of his brother on me from halfway across the room. His nostrils flare in an angry way. I don't dare move a muscle.

"Diego is dead?"

I nod emphatically and motion for my bloody front. "This is his blood. I stabbed him. H-He bled out all over me."

Esteban prowls closer until he's towering over me. Oscar tenses from beside me but makes no move to come between my monster and me. He leans forward and inhales me. Then, he pokes me hard in the chest.

"Ow!" I cry out and rub the spot.

He seizes my wrist, gripping it painfully. And still, Oscar doesn't intervene. Fucking pussy. "How are you certain he's dead?"

I swallow down my unease and focus on everything I practiced. Breaking down in front of the enemy wasn't part of the plan. I lift my chin and meet his dark brown glare. "I stabbed him in the heart. He bled out. I ran. There's no way he survived."

He twists my wrist until I yelp. When he sees the scar on the back of my hand, he roars. "He fucking scarred you?!"

Terror sends tears skating down my cheeks. Diego thinks I'm brave. It's an act. It's *all* an act. With him, I *am* brave because he's the hero in my story. But I'm terrified of the monster in this tale called *Life*.

"He made me his wife," I whisper, my bottom lip wobbling wildly. "Did you really think he would be good to me?"

Esteban runs his fingers through his slick black hair and snarls. "I don't know what I fucking thought." He turns to Oscar and slaps him on the side of the head. "This is all your fault."

Oscar rubs at his temple and glares at his brother. Esteban seems to shift his weight back and forth on his two feet, like a fighter who's about to go in for the kill. It makes me want to provoke him. Tell him exactly what his little brother did to me on the way here.

Not now.

"We got what we want and—" Oscar starts but Esteban silences him by punching him in the gut.

Oscar grunts but recovers quickly to scowl at his brother.

"Diego fucked me bare," I rattle out, my tone accusatory. "So many times. I'm probably riddled with diseases now." I don't meet Oscar's gaze. "I suffered. So much." A choked sob escapes me.

Esteban grabs my bicep and yanks me to him. I'm tugged into his powerful embrace. I feel as though I'm trapped in the arms of a bear. His touch is gentle as he strokes my hair.

"He better be dead, Roja," he murmurs against my hair.

Oscar's phone buzzes and soon he's whistling with excitement. "She did it. She really fucking did it!" He hands over his phone. I peer at the screen with Esteban. An unknown number texted him.

> **Unknown: That bitch killed him. We're coming for all of you.**
> **Unknown: VIDEO ATTACHED.**
> **Unknown: Watch this video because that is how we are going to kill every one of you.**

I shudder in Esteban's grip and he hugs me tighter. His scent suffocates me. At one time, I'd grown to anticipate it. I loved inhaling him. Now, I swear it makes me queasy. Just the thought of him on me and in me has me wanting to throw up all over this office.

Esteban presses play and the night before plays out exactly as rehearsed. The footage is from my old bedroom at me and Diego's home. To an outsider, it appears as though he chases me into the room and forces himself upon me.

Tears spill down my cheeks. He'd whispered that he loved me against my mouth just seconds before I had to hurt him. In the video, though, you don't hear those whispered words. You do see me slide my hand under the pillow to retrieve the short blade Diego gave to me to use.

"You really fucking did it," Oscar says, pride in his voice.

I stare in horror as I plunge the knife right into his chest. Tatiana had drawn an *X* with a Sharpie on Diego's chest—*and thank God the video is too grainy to see it*—so I wouldn't miss my intended target. I made sure it went exactly in the right way. She'd located a spot that she could easily fix and no vital organs or arteries would be harmed.

But it was still a gamble.

He could bleed to death.

I tremble as I wait for their sign. The video shows me throwing on clothes and bolting. Moments later, Jorge and Tatiana rush in. I can't look at Diego's unmoving form. My heart is seized up in my chest as I keep my gaze on Tatiana's hands.

"We've lost him!" she cries out.

But then it's there. A subtle motion of her thumb pointing up. That was the signal—the signal that meant he was going to be okay.

I let out a sigh and quickly follow it with, "I'm glad he's dead."

"How do they have this number?" Esteban demands waving the phone at me once the video is over. "They can track us."

"I-I must have left the number Oscar gave me there," I choke out. "I'm sorry."

He slams the phone to the tile floor and then stomps on

it until it's ruined. I wince because nobody will be tracking me that way now. Esteban shoos Oscar away. "Get lost. Me and Vee have some catching up to do."

Oscar clenches his jaw, shoots me a sad look, and turns to leave. To fucking leave. So much for stabbing Esteban in the back when he fucks me. I needed Oscar to kill Esteban for me. I know I can't take down Esteban, but I can sure as hell take down Oscar.

"Oscar," I murmur. He turns and gives me a slight shake of his head. Not now. Not fucking now. Pussy. I stand on my toes and whisper to Esteban. "Oscar forced himself on me this morning."

Esteban tenses and Oscar's mouth pops open in surprise.

"H-He has b-bad plans to kill you and take me for his own," I rattle out. "I d-don't want him. I w-want you." I'm shaking so bad I'm afraid I'll collapse.

Oscar's glare becomes murderous. "You traitorous bitch!"

He charges but doesn't get far before Esteban has him by the throat and against the wall. Esteban transforms into the beast he can be. Right now, he's a psychopathic one. His fist rears back and he slams it into his brother's face.

Crunch.

Crunch.

Crunch.

Over and over again.

So much blood.

I collapse to my knees, unable to take my eyes from the scene. If I don't stop him, Esteban will kill him. This is what I *want*. Right?

No. Not really. Not ever.

But this is what they made me *need*.

So with bile in my throat, I watch as one monster beats the other. Eventually, Esteban releases Oscar and he crumples to the floor. A part of me is disappointed to discover he's still alive. His sounds are gurgles and rasps. His teeth are broken and his nose is smashed. I'm sure more bones are broken, but I can't bear to look at his face anymore. It's too grotesque. He reaches for me, his hand touching my ankle, but I kick it away with a screech.

When Esteban yanks me up from the floor, I claw at him. Watching him hurt his own flesh and blood is a reminder that he's nothing but a horrific monster who will eventually kill me too.

"Stop!" he roars as he wrangles me into submission. His voice is softer. "We need to wash the blood off of both of us."

I'm helpless in his brutal grip as he drags me into the office bathroom. He locks the bathroom door behind us and stands between me and the door.

"Undress," he growls.

I shake my head at him. "No."

"I don't like that fire in your eyes," he hisses. "Undress."

Funny, because Diego loves my fire. "No."

His jaw clenches and his eyes turn nearly black with rage. This wasn't part of the plan. Oscar was supposed to kill him or at least give me the opportunity to do so. I wasn't supposed to provoke the beast.

Yet…here I am, telling him no.

I scream when he lunges for me. He tears my T-shirt straight from my body but my jeans take a little more work with me squirming. Eventually, after I'm naked, he rips away his own clothes and stalks me into the corner of the shower. I cower away from him, sobbing.

You endured months with this man.

You can endure a few more hours…

His hand grips my throat and he lifts me off my feet. I claw at his wrist, but he doesn't let me go. Ice-cold water suddenly showers down on me, causing me to shudder. He eases me back to my feet as the water warms but doesn't fully release my neck.

"Was it true? Diego fucked you bare? You could have fucking HIV or some shit?" he demands, spittle flying from his lips.

"Y-Yes," I hiss out.

He releases my throat some more. "And you could be pregnant with his child?"

My heart jackknifes in my chest. "N-No. They gave me birth control," I lie.

"Good," he snarls. "I'm not in the mood for a coat-hanger abortion today."

I shudder at his words but don't dare respond to that comment.

He grabs a bar of soap and begins aggressively scrubbing my body with it. I know he'll leave bruises by how forcefully he's pushing the bar against me. When he reaches my pussy with it, he stops to glare at me.

"My brother really fucked you?"

"Yes," I hiss.

"You didn't want it?" His tone is menacing.

"I didn't want it the last time either."

"What last time?" he demands through clenched teeth.

He starts scrubbing between my legs, and it hurts. The soap stings, and I squirm against it. I'm so focused on what he's doing that I barely realize he's asked me another question.

"I asked 'what last time,' goddammit!"

Pain slices through me when he rams the bar of soap inside of me. I choke and scream, but his grip on my throat tightens. His feral, evil face is inches from mine as he brutally fucks me with a bar of soap. It doesn't go deep, thank God, because he has it in his grip, but it goes deep enough to hurt really fucking bad.

I start to black out, my knees collapsing beneath me. The soap slips from his grip and hits the bottom of the shower with a thud. He pulls me into his arms to keep me from hitting the floor.

"What last time?" he asks, his tone much softer as he strokes my wet hair.

I'm shuddering in in his arms. "T-The n-night you t-t-took me to D-Diego's."

"That was me, Roja," he says with a chuckle.

I shake my head. "You stormed out and he...he..."

"He fucked you behind my back?" All humor is gone as the familiar possessiveness takes hold of his deep voice.

"Yes," I choke out. I'm overwhelmed and sick and hurting.

"Shhhh," he coos as he starts gently rinsing away all the soap. His hand cups my tender pussy as he rubs away the suds. Then, his fingers are inside of me, cleaning the soap out.

I'm in and out of a daze as he rinses me off. I barely register when he exits the shower to dress. I simply hug myself and sob as the water turns to ice. The water is turned off and Esteban stands before me, fully dressed.

"Time to go," he snaps.

I shiver uncontrollably and I can't tell if it's from the chill of the air or my nerves. "Where?"

I'm a stupid girl because I expect him to say "home."

"Time to break your fierce little spirit again. I was a fucking fool to let you go. You're mine, and they had no right touching you," he says in a low voice that makes my hair stand on end.

"Is he dead?"

He smirks. "He will be by the time I finish with him. He's not going anywhere, though. Little Oz won't be able to see after those hits to his face."

"Esteban," I start and hold a shaking hand up to him. "Please—"

He backhands me across the cheek, and I stumble into the wall. "At one time you worshipped the very ground I walked on."

I chance a look at him. He's rage personified. Nearly black eyes that glitter with evil. A clenched jaw that seems only seconds away from opening to devour me. "I'm sorry," I blurt out.

He shakes his head and his nostrils flare with fury. "We have a long road ahead of us, Roja. What was it last time? Four months?"

I fall to my knees and reach for him. "P-Please! No! I can't go in there again. I'll do whatever you want. Please, Esteban." My face throbs from where he hit me, but I keep my eyes on his. I try my hardest to summon the submissive look he's after.

He unbuckles his belt. If he wants to fuck me, so be it. Anything not to go back. But he whips off the belt instead with an elaborate swoosh. I can handle a spanking or a whipping or whatever else he has in mind with that thing. I can handle anything but being inside that container.

His entire body trembles with anger as he approaches. I close my eyes and await my punishment. The moment the leather tightens around my throat, I pop open my eyes in shock.

"W-What are you doing?"

"I'm reminding you who you belong to," he snaps and yanks the belt.

I fall forward and go to hold my hands out to stop me from crashing on my face, but then he yanks the belt high. I'm dragged to my feet while the belt cuts off my air supply. I grip the leather to try and free my throat so I can breathe to no avail. He drags me out of the bathroom, like I'm a fucking dog, and I'm powerless to fight against him.

He stalks past his abused and noisily breathing brother on the floor and out of the office. I'm naked and hurting and scared out of my mind. But there's no time to process any of it. All I can do is practically run after him to keep from getting choked to death. Several men with assault rifles glare at me with hunger in their eyes. When I get out of here, I'll kill them all.

Esteban *will* suffer.

Esteban *will* feel the pain he's caused me.

And I *will* get out of here.

XV | Diego

MY EYES ARE CLOSED BUT THE SMALL GIRL HUMS A SWEET *song from a Disney movie as she unpeels her Band-Aids and places them on my face. One by one. The birds chirp and a small breeze blows, but I'm too weak to open my eyes. Her hair must be long because it brushes against my arm. I'm numb. So numb. My mother is going to be so upset with me. That is, if I make it out of here alive. I'd gone into this dumb mission of mine a few months before my eighteenth birthday, thinking I'd steal the coke and make a quick sale to get her some medications she could take to make her feel better.*

And now...

Now I'm screwed.

Camilo, our country's biggest cartel leader, has all but gutted me. And if it weren't for this little girl, he would have succeeded.

With each passing second, I grow weaker. I never had any siblings, but I know that I would feel protective over them. Especially a little sister. This little girl—who can't be very old, based on the sound of her voice—is someone I will protect.

She continues humming, and I latch on to the sound of it.

Maybe I'm already dead. Maybe this is heaven. Maybe she's an angel.

The warm breath has her hair tickling my arm again. I suppose there are worse ways to die and worse places to end up. If I had to spend the rest of eternity in this moment, I could.

I'm at peace.

"Fuuuuck," I wake with a hiss and squint against a bright light. "What the fuck?" Pain throbs from my chest, and I'm disoriented. Am I almost eighteen again? Am I bleeding out on the grass?

"Diego," a familiar voice chokes out.

Is that my mother?

"I was so worried you wouldn't come to!"

I blink my eyes open, and Tatiana comes into focus. The fog dissipates and everything comes back to me like a ton of crushing bricks.

"Vienna," I snarl, ignoring the biting pain in my chest. "Where is Vienna?"

Jorge stalks over to the bedside. "She's with them. I watched her climb into the car with the youngest Rojas brother."

I scrub at my face but it pulls at my chest. When I look down, I can see I'm sporting fresh new stitches from where Vienna stabbed me. "What did you give me?" I demand.

Tatiana holds up her hand in protest. "Nothing, just like

you requested. However, you drank too much alcohol before this, which was not what I requested. It made your blood thinner, so you bled more. You're lightheaded from the blood loss but you'll be okay with rest."

"Rest?!" I hiss as I sit up. A blanket has been thrown over my waist but my cock is still sticky from being inside my wife recently. "How much time has passed?"

Jorge holds up his phone to show a tracker. "Almost two hours."

"Why didn't you fucking wake me up sooner?" I snarl and sling the sheet away, uncaring if they see my fucking cock. Tatiana reaches for me when I stumble, but I swat her away. "I'm fine. I need clothes and some goddamned coffee. And I need us to leave in the next five minutes."

I walk past Jorge and head toward my bedroom. Blindly, I grab a pair of holey jeans and a white T-shirt. Then, I throw on some socks and a pair of boots. Once I'm dressed, I storm into my office, feeling much clearer in the head. My chest hurts like a motherfucker, but I've received and lived through worse stab wounds.

"Where are they headed?"

"West. They haven't stopped," Jorge tells me. He begins checking his weapons.

I locate my Glock and holster. The movement is painful, but I finally get it strapped to my back under my shirt. My favorite knife gets hooked to my belt, and I snag my cigar from the ashtray. Once it's ready and lit, I inhale a plume of smoke and motion for the door.

"Let's go," I order, the cigar wiggling between my teeth.

He follows me out and Tatiana meets me in the hall. Her medical bag is on one shoulder and she holds a thermos in her hand.

"You shouldn't be smoking, Diego." When I glower at her, she quickly continues. "Coffee. And I have food in my bag for you to eat along the way." She lifts her chin bravely. "I'm coming with you."

I shake my head as I storm past her. "Fuck no."

"Diego! Yes!" she hollers after me. "You're not well, and I need to make sure you remain okay. And what if…" she trails off. "I need to be there for Vee."

I freeze at her words. She's right. Vienna and I discussed this at great lengths. I was sickened as she detailed out every single thing Esteban and Oscar had ever done to her. There was more of the same where they were concerned. We both knew this going into our plan. If she hadn't been so god-damned adamant, I'd have told her the fuck with her plan.

But my scarlet-headed vixen?

Nobody tells mi diablita no.

Not even me.

You let her wreak her havoc.

She's a storm and a hell-raiser.

And I have her back, which is why we need to get the hell on the road.

"Let's go," I bark out. "I want more men on this with us."

Jorge nods and pulls out his cell to make his orders. As we climb into Jorge's SUV, I notice several of my men emerge from the tree line, assault rifles in hand.

"They're right behind us," he assures me as we tear off down the driveway.

I set my cigar down in the ashtray and regard my right-hand man. "Where do you think they're going?" I ask and twist my wedding ring around my finger.

Jorge scrubs his face. "I don't fucking know."

I pull out my phone and call my little American friend. She answers on the first ring.

"Is Vee okay?" she blurts out in greeting.

"She will be if you continue to uphold your end of the deal, cariño," I grumble. Getting her to help me was like pulling fucking teeth. Eventually, she pulled the strings I needed her to because a deal is a deal and, like me, she's not one to break her word. "Is your boyfriend's dad still tracking the earrings?"

She swallows loudly into the phone. "He is. We're watching it on the monitor now. It's moving in the same direction as the phone. Oscar and Vee are together." She lets out a teary sob. "How could he do this to her?"

I don't remind her that he's a fucking Rojas. He's not my friend. Oscar is the scum on the bottom of my shoe. "It doesn't matter," I snap. "He did it. He's probably still fucking doing it. I want you to call me if anything changes on the GPS location of either trace."

"Of course," she breathes. "Diego…bring my friend back home. I can tell you care about her. It surprises me that you care about anyone but yourself, but apparently you do. You looked after and protected me. I know you'll do the same for her. Thank you."

My chest tightens. A year ago, I'd have laughed if someone would have told me I'd befriend a little feisty American and marry her even feistier best friend. "I love her, Gabriella."

She sniffles. "I know you do."

We hang up and Tatiana shoves a sandwich in my face. "Eat. You need the protein."

Jorge snorts, and I roll my eyes as I take the sandwich. I

chomp on it but it only reminds me of my wife. That fucker never fed her. Fucking sandwiches like once a day. Bile rises in my throat at the thought of him torturing her further. I swallow down my bite and then toss the sandwich out the window. Tatiana grumbles, but I ignore her as I chug down the hot coffee instead. Once I'm feeling better, I prepare my cigar and relight it, sticking it between my teeth. Nothing will bring me comfort right now, but this is a start.

Be brave, mi amor.

Be fucking brave.

I jolt awake at the sound of my phone ringing. "Yes?"

"The cell phone is gone. They must have destroyed it," Gabriella tells me, her voice urgent. "The earrings are still picking up a signal. But Diego?"

"What?" I demand.

"They've been stopped at the same location for the past fifteen minutes. It's a location we know…"

"And?"

"Buenaventura. Camilo's old shipyard."

I seethe into the phone. "You mean my new shipyard."

"They're there. If it's yours, why haven't your men called to tell you?" she questions.

Because I've been fucking betrayed. I should have known Esteban and Oscar would have been able to sway some of their old men. "Call me if anything changes," I bark at her before hanging up.

"What is it?" Jorge demands.

"Buenaventura. They've taken over. Alert our men," I growl. "We're about to fucking go to war."

We're still two hours behind when Vienna left with Oscar. It pains me knowing she'll be in their custody for two minutes, much less two hours. My wife is strong and brilliant and tougher than nails but...

Esteban is fucking crazy.

Fury bubbles up inside of me. The men who betrayed me will all die. One by one, I will end them all. I'll save Esteban for last. I'll slice him up, like I sliced up his father. The Rojas fucks will be nothing but shit on the sole of my shoes when I'm finished with them.

I unsheathe my blade and it glints in the morning light. I'm going to fuck them all up. Nobody hurts my wife and lives to tell about it. Fucking nobody.

"This is such a bad idea," Tatiana complains from the backseat. "Ever since you met this girl, your life has been topsy turvy."

I inhale a sharp breath. "Ever since I met her, my life has come into focus. I love her and I'd take a million stabs to the chest if it means I'll get to have her in the end. Vienna is a flame I want to get burned by, don't you see? I don't want to feel safe and secure if I can't have her. I'd much rather live and die fighting as long as I can do it with her."

Tatiana reaches forward and clutches my shoulder. "I just worry about you."

I turn and give her a wicked grin. "You should worry about them. They're all about to be slaughtered."

She frowns and nods. "I knew that day you showed up on my operating table that you'd be trouble. And yet..." she trails off and flashes me a proud smile. "You're always worth it because you're the boy I could never have."

Warmth floods my chest, and I close my eyes as we continue our drive. My mother would be proud of me. Not for the cartel shit and all that comes with it. She'd be proud of me for loving Vienna and finding a motherly friend in Tatiana. Integrity was always a big deal for my mother, which is why I've always kept my word in every situation. "A man's word is his honor," she'd said. I'm sure she'd be proud of the man I've become.

Now I need to continue to live up to her expectations.

I'll fulfil them all.

And that starts with rescuing my queen.

I'm coming, mi diablita. Just hold on for me, beautiful.

XVI | Vee

A S SOON AS THE RUSTY OLD CONTAINER COMES INTO VIEW,
I know that's where we're going. Intuition, if you will.
Esteban had put me in one like it once before. Hidden
away in the back of the lot where nobody would hear my
screams.

"No!"

He yanks on the belt, and I stumble forward. I tug at the
leather but it's so tight, I can't even get my finger between it
and my throat. I'm hissing for air when I'm dragged into the
dark unit. Panic washes over me. My heart races so fast in my
chest, I'm afraid I'll black out. Memories of so many months
locked away threaten to consume me. I can't do this again.

Diego.

Diego will find you.

Breathe.

The door is left open behind us and Esteban shoves me
toward the back. I fall to my knees but I take the moment to
yank the belt from my throat and toss it away. The morning

sunlight shines in and illuminates the space. But not for long. Never for long. Soon it will be nothing but me and the darkness. His heavy footsteps thunder behind me. He wants to corner me, and like the scared little animal I am right now, I run straight for the corner as if it will offer me an escape.

My knees land on a dilapidated mattress. It's then when I realize he was going to put me in here whether or not I behaved. A sick game to him. Breaking me is his brand of fun. Fire blazes inside my chest, and I turn to face my attacker. When he nears, I kick him and the bottom of my heel slams onto his jaw. Pain rips up my foot, but it knocks him off his game for a second. I scramble past him, but he hooks me around my waist.

"Not so fast," he snarls against my hair. "You need to calm the fuck down, Roja."

He tries to pry open my mouth, and instead of fighting him, I open and then bite down hard.

"FUCKING CUNT!" he roars as he rips at my hair.

I release him and cry out. I'm tossed down onto the mattress. Before I can move, he tackles me. I squirm, but he wrangles me onto my back. He pins my body with his massive weight and binds my wrists together with one hand.

"Open," he orders.

I shake my head.

"So help me," he snarls, his spit showering down on me, "if you don't open your goddamned mouth, I'll cut your tongue out and shove it up your ass."

A shudder ripples through me.

But I open my goddamned mouth.

He shoves a pill deep into my mouth until I'm forced to swallow it. I know what it is. Same hazy drug from last time.

With the sun shining in from the doorway, it casts a shadow on his face, but illuminates him from behind.

A demon.

Esteban was sent straight from where nightmares are made to torment me in this life.

One day, I'll send him back to hell.

He holds me in his tight grip until my eyelids grow heavy and I give in to exhaustion. Fifteen minutes pass, maybe longer, but the drug is taking effect. When he realizes I've relaxed, he releases my hands. They're throbbing but a buzzing has already begun to course through me.

I hate this feeling.

"I missed you," he tells me, his voice a low growl that echoes through every nerve ending in my body.

I shiver and squirm. My body is pulsating, especially between my legs. "Fuck you," I murmur.

He slaps me hard across the face. The sting of it zings through my body and feels as though it ricochets off every inch of my flesh. I'm still reeling when he stands up. I hear the jangle of his belt even before I see it. With a quickness I can barely register, he binds my wrists with the leather.

The only thing he can do that he hasn't done already is kill me.

And as psycho as Esteban is, I don't think he has it in him. He'd much rather keep me as his toy to torment.

"Your pussy still belongs to me," he tells me as he clutches my knees and pries them apart.

I don't have the strength to fight against him. The more I fight, the more he hurts me. I knew this was what would happen. I ensured Diego I could handle it.

I *can* handle it.

But after today, I won't have to handle it ever again.

"Did Oscar make you come?" he asks, his long finger dragging a trail from my belly button down south. He stops right before he reaches my clit. "Hmm?"

"N-No," I rasp out. My duplicitous body shudders with need. Those fucking pills are the devil.

"Good. That kid got more pussy than anyone I know, but can you imagine how many unsatisfied girls are out there?" he questions. His finger circles my clit, and I jolt in response. "Now me…" he trails off, his dark eyes finding mine. "Every girl I touch comes without fail. Your mother came many times for me."

He's fucking with me.

I hope.

"I hate you," I tell him but my hips are lifting as if they're drawn like a magnet to him.

"Hate is just as intense as love." He rubs my clit with his one finger. My entire body thrums with pleasure. If I could escape my body, I'd find a way to choke him with his belt. "You like this, don't you? When I touch you this way?"

Tears roll out and I shake my head. But my quivering body says otherwise.

"Lies, Roja. Your cunt is dripping."

My body is sore from his brutalization in the shower, but it doesn't stop the need from coursing through me. He slides his finger down my seam and he barely pushes the tip of it inside me.

"Wet," he tells me. "Don't worry. You don't have to be ashamed. What we have is beautiful."

His finger inches in slowly, stretching my bruised flesh. I groan when he easily pushes another finger inside me.

"I'm going to make you come," he tells me in a smug tone. "And then I'm going to wrap my cock up so you don't give me any goddamned diseases so I can fuck that needy pussy until you scream. You want that, Roja?"

"Fuck you," I whisper. "Oh God…"

Pleasure zings through me and I'm confused. The haze he likes to cloud me with is intense. As much as I hate him, I feel like my body needs the pleasure. I close my eyes when he starts kissing his way down my stomach.

Diego.

Lightest brown eyes I've ever seen.

Charming and sexy to a fault.

Mine. Mine. Mine.

Esteban's mouth latches on to my clit and he begins sucking as he finger-fucks me slowly. I hate that he steals me away from thoughts of my husband. Every part of my body is on fire. It feels good. So wrong but good.

One day I'll make him pay for all of this.

Even in my haze, I realize these sensations coursing through me are induced by the drugs. With Diego, they're real. He doesn't have to drug me to get me to come. I want every part of him.

Esteban has dedicated his life to being nothing but a low-life cheater.

He steals what he wants but doesn't deserve a thing.

Someone screams, jerking me from my thoughts. I realize this person is me as an unwanted orgasm cuts through me. At one time, emotion had been attached to them but now it's nothing more than physiological.

Find me, Diego.

I close my eyes when Esteban slips his fingers out of me

and unzips his pants. The tear of the condom wrapper makes me shudder, but I don't dare watch him. He spreads my knees apart so that he can worm his hulk-like body between them.

And then he's hammering one more nail into his coffin. By taking me again, he's sentencing himself to a painful death. This foolish man fell for the bait. I walked right into his trap so that I could annihilate him from the inside out.

"Look at me," he hisses as he thrusts painfully into me.

I pop my eyes open, ignoring the bruises inside of me, and glare at him. "You're going to die."

He fucks me so hard I scream, but I stare him down with the promise of a long, torturous death glimmering in my eyes. The sick fucker must like it because he comes with a grunt.

Pop! Pop! Pop!

"What the fuck?" he snarls as he stiffens. He yanks out of me and shoves his still sheathed dick inside his pants. "What did you do?"

His accusation makes me start laughing.

"I fucked *you*!" I screech. My body is numb and tingling but fire blazes within me. "You're going to die."

He grabs my jaw and then turns my head forcefully to the right. A scream rips through me when he snatches the diamond stud out of my earlobe. "You set me up!" he roars. "You fucking set me and my brother up!"

Pain radiates from my torn ear, but I find the energy to spit in his face. "Damn right I did."

He stands and yanks me to my feet by my hair. I'm dragged beside him toward the door when a shadow steps in front of the doorway. My heart leaps at the sight of him.

Lean and fierce.

Terrifyingly beautiful.

My partner and lover.

My husband.

"Diego," I moan.

I can't make out his facial features because the sun streaming in is too bright, but by the way his shoulders heave, I can tell he's infuriated.

"Don't move or I'll cut her throat wide open," Esteban threatens. A blade pokes my flesh, hard enough that he breaks the skin.

"Always such a pussy," Diego growls. "Just like your father. Always picking on those smaller than you."

Esteban drags the knife along my flesh, tearing the skin along the way. It isn't deep but it hurts, even through my drugged state. "You're going to kill me anyway, so I may as well take her with me."

Diego remains calm and still. His blade glints in the sunlight. "She's not yours to take. Never was. Vienna has always been mine. Since before she ever laid eyes on you. Fate, they call it. And you're about to meet yours."

"She belongs to me, but you tried to take that, too," Esteban snarls. "Just like you took my father's life."

Diego takes a step into the container. "Let her go and fight like a fucking man. At least your father had the balls to do that much."

Esteban growls and he hugs me possessively. The knife digs a little deeper into my flesh.

"Do you want to go to your grave like a pussy or do you want to go with some dignity?" Diego taunts.

Esteban stiffens. "I've killed many men. I'll kill you too."

Diego laughs and it warms me to my soul. "You can

fucking try."

To my surprise, Esteban shoves me to the floor. I go down hard on my knees, and the container echoes with the sound. Diego's eyes never fall to me. His eyes are locked on his target. Esteban practically huffs like a bull trapped in a cage. Ready to charge at any second.

"Did you fuck my wife?" Diego questions as he quickly tears off his T-shirt and tosses it my way.

Esteban laughs like a madman. "I fucked her good. She'll be feeling me inside her cunt for days."

Diego's frame is thinner—solid lean muscle compared to Esteban's hulkish build. He bounces from foot to foot, like a graceful dancer, while Esteban throbs with barely contained rage. With shaking hands, I pull the shirt on over me and inhale the scent of my man.

"You won't touch her ever again," Diego hisses and waves his knife in front of him in a fluid motion.

Esteban hisses and jumps back. "Motherfucker!"

Blood soaks the front of his shirt, and I smile. I hope he makes him fill up this entire container with his blood.

"Pussy," Diego hisses and bounces forward on his toes. Slash. And then he bounces back. Esteban groans but waves his knife out in front of him in defense. Diego has already moved out of reach. His eyes stay on his target but his presence is like a warm hug.

"Your family name is a disgrace," Diego tells him.

Esteban lunges for him with his knife raised. Diego does some fancy arm movements before ducking around him. Now he stands between me and the monster. My hero.

"You run out that door and they'll mow you down with every bullet in their arsenal," Diego warns with a laugh.

I want to wrap my arms around my husband, but he needs to stay focused. Esteban charges again, but Diego slashes him across his face with the knife. A groan rips from Esteban and he drops to his knees. His knife clatters to the metal floor, and he clutches the wound that is gushing blood.

Diego pounces like a stealthy cat and grabs a handful of Esteban's hair while pressing his blade to his carotid artery.

"Mi diablita," he hisses my way. "What do you want me to do? I can end this now…"

I stand on shaky legs and wobble toward them. "Or I can."

His beautiful eyes meet mine, and I almost collapse under the weight of the love shining in them. I bend over and retrieve Esteban's abandoned knife. His enraged glare meets mine from his kneeling position.

"Just kill me," he snarls. "Fucking kill me, Roja."

Diego rips harder at his hair. "Don't talk to your queen like that, motherfucker."

I narrow my eyes at Esteban but speak to my husband. "Are his wounds lethal?"

"All superficial at this point," he growls.

I smile. "Good."

Esteban's evil face scrunches into one of confusion. "You're going to let me live?"

I bend over and glower at him. "I'm going to break you."

"What the fuck, Vee?" Esteban demands. For the first time in my entire life, I see fear in the monster's eyes. Fear of me.

"What do you think, baby?" I ask Diego. "Four months? Is that long enough?"

189

"FUCKING KILL ME NOW!" Esteban screams. "NOW!"

I kick him hard in the balls, and with the drugs still buzzing in my body, I nearly come from the way he screeches in pain. The sound of his pain is beautiful. Four months isn't nearly long enough.

"I want to keep him right here. I want him to relive every single second of what I went through. Put his piece of shit brother in here after you make sure he's dead so he can be forced to live with that rotting scent every hour of every day." My eyes dart to Diego's. "I want him to pay. Dying is too easy."

Diego slashes his knife along the back of Esteban's calves through his slacks. Esteban's screams are otherworldly. When Diego releases him, Esteban falls to his side as he clutches his calves.

"He's not leaving this container on his two feet," Diego assures me with a wicked gleam in his eyes. "I'll station a trusted man at the door. Whatever you want, mi diablita, we'll make it happen."

While Esteban writhes in pain, I wobble over to Diego. He's shaking, and I wonder if it's from anger or from the wound that's seeping blood on his chest. I wince upon realizing he's torn some stitches.

"A hero would carry his queen right out of here," he says with a grunt, his fingers brushing through my tangled hair.

I grip his hand with mine and tug him toward the door. "Good thing we're villains because we're going to walk out of here together. Equals. King and queen. Heroes are for fairy-tales." I rest my head on his shoulder. "Our story is one from the horror section."

He kisses the top of my head. "With a little erotica thrown in?"

I laugh as we slowly make our way into the bright sunlight. "With a lot of erotica thrown in."

His palm finds my face and he kisses me hard. "I love you."

"I love you more."

XVII | Diego

"I'M SO EXHAUSTED," VIENNA MURMURS AS SHE SHAKILY makes her way to our bed. We've been home for only a few hours. Long enough to feed our starving bodies and for me to wash every inch of the scum from her. My sweet wife cried for a short while in the shower but her quiet strength didn't allow the tears to fall for long. I can't begin to imagine what she's going through right now.

"Let's sleep." I turn off the lights and join my naked woman in the bed. She feels warm and soft in my grip. I'm thankful I can't see her bruises and lacerations in the dark. "I'm so sorry."

She stiffens in my arms. "For what?"

"For today. I know we talked about everything that would happen. But planning it and going through with it are two different things. I should never have agreed," I grit out.

Her palm slides up my bare chest but avoids the stitched flesh. "I didn't give you a choice."

I lean forward and kiss her somewhere on her face. "I should have told you no."

She scoffs. "As if I would have listened."

"I could have made you see a different way," I growl. "It didn't have to end with two men—your two enemies—raping and beating you, goddammit."

"It was the only way," she murmurs. "I was the bait."

I'm still unsettled but I know she won't back down on this. We spoke for hours while setting up this plan. She told me in detail what they would do to her based on what they'd done before. My fiery Vienna wanted this. Her claws were bared and ready to exact damage. She just needed to get inside their den first.

It still pisses me off that their "den" was my goddamned port. Several of the men turned against me for the Rojas brothers. Those men are dead now. But Ricardo and many others refused to sell out. They'd been tortured. Some killed. When Jorge discovered them in another shipping container, it took three men to hold Ricardo back from trying to kill Esteban. But once Vienna explicitly asked him what she needed him to do for her, Ricardo wholeheartedly agreed.

Ricardo is Esteban's warden now.

Except when Vienna comes to visit.

Until then, Ricardo will feed him sandwiches once a day. He'll change out his piss bucket once a week, if he's lucky. And he's not, under any circumstances, allowed to talk to Esteban. But he is allowed to fuck him. Ricardo's exact words were, "His ass is mine."

Esteban is getting to see exactly what he put Vienna through.

A severe and fitting punishment.

One of the men was instructed to finish off Oscar, if he was still alive, and put his body in with Esteban. Esteban could smell his brother as he decayed just as Vienna was forced to smell her mother.

An eye for a motherfucking eye.

"How long do you think he'll live?" she whispers, hate giving her voice a slight edge.

"Tatiana cleaned his wounds and stitched him up. Ricardo has been instructed not to hurt him more than necessary. I suppose he'll live as long as you want him to," I tell her and brush my fingers through her hair.

"I don't want him to die easy. This punishment will satisfy me until I can come up with something better." She cuddles against me and presses her lips to my jaw. "Thank you for trusting me. Together we did this." Her palm cups my face and the metal from her wedding ring, which she put back on, cools my face.

"We're going to do so much more together," I assure her. "Together we're going to rule our little corner of the fucking world."

She lets out a contented sigh. "Nobody will mess with us. And if they try, we'll make them pay."

I chuckle and twist my finger in her hair before tugging it in a playful way. "So you're into torturing now? You're barely a cartel queen, yet here you are so goddamned serious about your job. I love your drive, mi diablita."

She laughs too and then we're both quiet.

The exhaustion of the day steals us from our moment, but at least we enter the dream world in each other arms. Just like everything else we do. Together. Side by side.

Three months later...

"How's our little captive?" I ask Ricardo on speakerphone.

He laughs and it's evil as hell. "His ass is a little sore and the big fucker has lost some major weight, but he's hanging in there."

I smirk. "I thought you were into the ladies."

Ricardo grunts. "The ladies get plenty of Ricardo. But Ricardo puts his dick wherever he wants."

"Don't tell me every Colombian asshole around here speaks of himself in third person," Vienna groans from my office doorway.

I motion for her to come sit in my lap. My stunning bride wears a short tank top dress that barely hits the top of her thighs. Too short. She likes to torment me while I work.

"My little Vienna," Ricardo greets, a smile in his voice. "How is my little hellraiser? Already time for another visit?"

She chuckles as she straddles my lap. "You just want to show off again. We all know you're amazing at butt sex," she teases.

They chat a bit while I grab her hips and make her rub her pussy against my cock through our clothes. Vienna gets a little too eager when they talk torture. One day, once the pain of what Esteban did to her settles, she'll probably ease off a bit. But as it stands, at least once a week, we drive out to Buenaventura for a visit. She makes Ricardo bind Esteban and then fuck him in front of her. And whenever she's in charge, Ricardo makes it real nice for Esteban. Just like Esteban used to do for her. He pleasures the straight man until Esteban is coming with a big Colombian meathead deep in his ass. Every visit ends with a kiss to the top of Esteban's head before she kicks him in the balls. It's funny as fuck.

"Is our first shipment to San Diego ready to go?" I question.

He grunts. "Will be in the next day or so. You'll have plenty of time to get to the States and sort out your business before the shipment arrives."

We talk a little while longer before we hang up. The moment he's off the phone, my gorgeous wife mauls me. Her mouth attacks mine and she starts tugging at my tie.

"This. Off. Now," she orders between kisses.

Ignoring her request, I lift her dress up off her body and then discard it. My naughty little thing isn't wearing anything under her dress. This makes my cock really fucking hard.

"You're so bad," I growl.

She laughs and leans back so I can regard her swollen tits. They're tender these days and my fucking God are they huge. I lean forward and tongue one of her nipples.

"These are so goddamned beautiful," I praise.

Her fingers undo my tie and she tosses it away. Then, she is on a quick mission to unbutton my vest. "Why do you wear so many clothes?" she complains.

I chuckle and reach between us to rub on her clit. "I like to tease you, mi diablita. I like to watch you go hungry for my cock."

She licks her plump bottom lip and it makes my dick thump against her. "I'm always hungry for your cock. Especially when you're naked. You should be naked more often."

I lift an eyebrow at her. "This is just the hormones talking."

A few weeks after we came back, Vienna learned she was

pregnant. Tatiana said we probably conceived during the week after our wedding. I've been walking around with my chest filled with pride since the moment two little blue lines showed up on that stick. It's been surreal thus far but lately, her flat stomach has begun to protrude with our child. She's hot as fuck carrying my baby.

"Shut up and take your clothes off already," she orders with a wicked smile. "Momma needs Daddy's fat cock inside her."

I growl because I love when she talks dirty to me. My little wife knows this and uses it like a weapon. Together we're all but ripping my clothes off me.

"Beg Daddy Diego for his anaconda."

She snorts. "Put that big snake in me, Daddy."

I lift her by her hips and plop her on the edge of my desk while I push down the rest of my clothes. She's fucking glorious to look at with her brilliant red hair and blazing green eyes. Her tits are carved from God's finest materials. And she's mine. All mine.

"Show me your needy cunt. I want to see how it weeps for me," I mumble as I stroke my dick.

Her eyes fall to my cock and she grins before leaning back on my desk. She puts her feet on the edge of the desk so that her pussy is on full display. Then, she slides her fingers down her cute belly and touches her clit. Our eyes find each other as we pleasure ourselves. My cock aches to get the fuck out of my hand and into this gorgeous woman.

"Is it wet for me?"

She nods and pushes a finger inside her body. When she removes it, it glistens with her arousal. I lean forward so she can slip it into my mouth. I suck off her sweet taste. My God, this woman makes me horny as fuck. I can be having a shit day, yet one look at her supple body and all is forgotten.

"Beg for it."

"Please," she whines, "give me your cock. Fuck me good and hard."

I groan in pleasure. Her words are like fucking fire. They burn me in the best possible way. Everything in me buzzes to slam into her, but I like making her wait. I like seeing her arousal leak from her body.

I reach forward and swat her hand away so I can take over touching her clit. She can come at her own touch, but she goes fucking crazy when I do it for her. I thought that after all that happened with Esteban and Oscar a few months ago, she'd be gun shy. But my woman is tough as shit because as soon as her body healed, she was all over me, begging for my cock. Each time I'm inside her, it's just one more time they won't ever be.

"Diego," she murmurs. "Oh, God…"

Her body writhes as I bring her pleasure. I rub her faster and smile when the opening of her pussy shimmers in the light. Like a fucking magical unicorn, this cunt of hers. I'll ride it all the way to hell.

"You ready for Daddy D's big cock?"

"Yessss," she moans.

"When you come, I'll put my dick inside you. Come, beautiful."

It takes her another few moments, but soon she's crying out my name. I make good on my promise the moment she stops jolting in pleasure and tease her wet entrance with the tip of my cock. Vienna doesn't like it slow often. Usually, at night, she'll let me make love to her. But during the day, in my office, is the time reserved for hard fucking.

With a growl, I slam into my wife so hard, the desk scrapes against the wood floors. She cries out and fondles her tender breasts. I almost come, imagining my son or daughter latched onto one in the near future.

Fucking Vienna is the best reward this life has given me. Nothing else in this world matters. Not this giant house. Not my empire. Not this country. Just her. We could be poor and living in a shack on the other side of the world and I'd be happy as a fucking lark to have her in my bed and in my heart.

"Come here, mi amor," I growl as I pull her into my arms. Her legs wrap around my waist when I lift her. I prefer having her big tits pressed against me when my dick is inside her. But mostly, I want her mouth on mine.

She kisses me hard as I sit back in my chair. We settle into a position where she can ride me. I tangle my fingers in her hair and give her love bites all over her throat until her telling whimpers warn me of an upcoming orgasm.

"I love you," I murmur against her flesh.

Her fingers run through my hair and she moans. "I love you too."

Her cunt clenches hard around me a second before she screams out my name. I let out a guttural groan as I blow my load deep inside of her. We're both breathing raggedly as we come down from our high.

"So this is the life, huh?" she asks, burying her face against the side of my neck. "It doesn't get any better than this."

I grin and hug her tight. It jostles her enough that I feel my cum run back down the side of my cock to the chair below me. "This is everything, baby."

XVIII | Vee

I CHEW ON MY BOTTOM LIP AS I STARE UP AT THE NICE home through the windshield. We've been in San Diego for three weeks now, and I still haven't found the nerve to see Brie. I'm not sure why, but I feel like our friendship is broken. How do two wronged teenage girls who were forced to grow up way too fast find their way back together?

She knows everything.

I know she knows.

I've heard Diego talking to her on the phone. It's definitely me, not her. She wants to repair our friendship. And if it weren't for Diego forcing me to see her, I'd have chickened out.

I don't think twice about barking out orders to men three times my size who carry assault weapons, but when it comes to facing my best friend, I am weak.

"Are we going to sit in her driveway all day?" Diego asks, his palm resting on my thigh.

I turn to regard him and shrug. "Maybe."

He smirks and relaxes in his seat. "Take all the time you need. I'm on vacation."

I roll my eyes, but it's true. Diego has let me handle all of my father's affairs and has only stepped in when I've needed him. Together we made sure we fortified our shipyard here in California, but he let me be the one to boss everyone around. Most of the men have known me since I was a kid, so they weren't opposed to being under my leadership. The Gomez empire has come together over the past few months because we've done it together as partners.

And just like usual, he's waiting until I'm ready.

We go in together.

I'm still deep in thought when someone beats on my window with their fist. I shriek in surprise, and Diego already has a gun drawn from his belt aimed across me at our attacker. When I meet the familiar face of my ex-boyfriend, I swat Diego's arm away.

"Calder," I cry out, surprisingly happy to see him.

He pulls open the car door and tugs me into his arms. His hug is strong. Much different than I remember.

"When did you get so big?" I tease.

He chuckles and shrugs when we pull apart. "Probably about the same time you did."

We both look down at my growing belly and smile.

Calder's grin falls when a dark shadow comes up behind me. His eyes lift and worry flickers in them.

"Clader, this is my husband, Diego."

He nods and holds his hand out to shake Diego's. Diego shakes his hand but then points near the garage door. "Who's she?"

"Luciana," Calder says, pride in his voice. "My fiancée."

Her cheeks turn pink as she hesitantly makes her way over to him. He wraps a possessive arm around her before hugging her to him.

"Fiancée, huh?" I say with a grin. "Wow. Congrats."

"Nice to meet you," Diego says.

She gives him a shy wave.

"You can't speak?" He snorts. "What's the matter? Cat got your tongue?"

"A cat named Esteban," Calder growls.

A silent understanding blankets the air around us.

Luciana begins using her hands to speak in sign language. Calder translates for us.

"He cut out my tongue. I thought he ruined my life. But then I met a stunning sex god named Calder the Great." As soon as he says the last line, she swats at him and grumbles. Her sign language goes faster but he translates quickly to keep up. *"I didn't say that. Calder is just being Calder. We recently took a sign language course together so we could communicate but he gets lost in translation sometimes. I'm so happy you came to see Brie. She talks about you all the time."* Her nose crinkles and she points at Diego. *"You too."*

"How do you two kiss?" Diego questions point blank.

I elbow him in the side, but he simply winks at me.

Luciana raises her hands to answer, but Calder decides to show us instead. His fingers slide into her hair and he tilts her head up. Her black lashes bat shyly at him but she parts her mouth open in anticipation. Their lips press together softly at first but then he kisses her hard. Nothing about their kiss from the outside appears abnormal. Just possessive and consuming and filled with love. It makes my heart threaten to burst. Calder was always a good guy, but he was meant for a good girl.

I was a villain.

And I finally found my match.

When they finish their public display of affection, Calder motions us inside. "The food will be shit. Just warning you right now. Brie can cook macaroni and that's it. Ren knows how to heat up the leftovers we bring over. If we didn't live at the end of the street, these two knuckleheads would starve. Let's just pray they ordered pizza. So help me if Brie tries to make enchiladas again…"

Luciana groans and holds her stomach. "Ew."

Calder reaches for the door when it swings open. Ren, a giant version of the guy I remember, stands in the doorway with a baby swaddled in a pink blanket in his arms. All apprehension fades away the moment I see the baby.

"Oh my God!" I screech as I run straight to him and give him a quick hug. "Is this Alejandra?"

He chuckles. "We call her Ally for short but yes. Fussy as fuck."

I playfully swat his stomach and steal the sweet infant from him. Her big nearly black eyes stare up at me. I love her and she isn't even mine. "You're so beautiful. You and your brother are going to be best friends with our little baby."

Ally lets out a big sigh, and I laugh.

"Come inside," Ren says with a chuckle. "Brie's feeding little D right now."

I peer over my shoulder and Diego stands in the threshold with stiff shoulders. Ren's gaze drifts to his and his jaw clenches.

"Bygones, man," Ren says, if anything a little begrudgingly. "You're married to one of my good friends and she's happy. Let's move forward."

Diego told me of his previous flirtations and advances with Brie. He said he was like that with all women until I put his balls in my purse forever. Such a romantic, that guy.

"Come on, babe," I tell him and walk inside.

The house smells good. Like something has been cooking all day. Calder saunters past me tugging Luciana behind him and hollers. "What is this sorcery?"

Brie rounds the corner with another brown-haired baby, but this one is latched to her breast. She sees Calder first and sticks her tongue out at him. "I can read directions, asshole. Luci gave me a crockpot recipe to try. Shut your pie hole and eat my food or I'll make you change the twins next time they have a monster diaper blowout."

He gags which makes Ren snort with laughter. These people, my friends from ages ago, are happy. Happy looks good on them. Diego wraps an arm around me and kisses the top of my head. It's then that Brie sees us. Her smile falls as tears well in her eyes.

"Vee."

She walks over to me and we stare at each other, both of us with babies in our arms. Silly tears sneak out of my eyes as I regard my friend. I thought it would be weird, but mostly I'm just happy to see her.

"You look well," she tells me with a huge grin. "Is this punk still being good to you?"

Diego chuckles and the deep rumble warms me to my soul. "I'm good to her every single night, cariño. So good. I think even the people three towns over can vouch for how good I am to her."

Brie snorts and shakes her head. "I forgot how perverted

you are."

"I highly doubt that," he retorts.

Ally starts fussing and Ren comes to the rescue. He's big and bulky now but the way he looks at the babies melts my heart. I wonder if Diego will regard our future children with such a brilliant look of raw love.

I know so.

As soon as he walks away with the baby, Brie's eyes bug out. "YOU'RE PREGNANT?!" she screeches which makes baby Duvan jump in surprise.

Diego hugs me from behind and palms my belly. "Mi familia."

She shakes her head but beams at us. "Would you look at us? We're all grown up now."

"But Vienna still likes to call me daddy," Diego says as his teeth nip at my ear.

Brie laughs. "Oh my God. I don't even know how you put up with him, but I'm glad you're happy, Vee."

She reaches her hand for mine and I take it. Of course I take it. Brie is my best friend. Some shit happened, some time happened, and some distance happened. But our friendship still exists. A sturdy tree that still stands after one helluva hurricane.

As she pulls me toward the living room, I can't help but make sure my other half is coming with me. Where I go, he goes. We're two halves of a very perfect whole. His lips are quirked up into an amused smile. I love how his light brown eyes seem to twinkle with mischief.

With my best friend tugging me along and my husband having my back, I can't help but think life doesn't get any better.

I feel a tiny nudge in my stomach and it reminds me.

The best is yet to come.

"I can have Dan update me by phone. We don't have to go," Diego says, his black brows furled together in concern.

I reach over and brush his black hair out of his eye. "We need to go. The new shipment arrived late last night, and we need to make sure everything goes smoothly. These first few shipments are important."

He frowns. "But you're sick, Vienna."

Bile rises in my throat, and I wince. The morning sickness, I thought, was supposed to end after my first trimester. But Tatiana tells me some women are lucky to have bouts of it throughout their entire pregnancy. Today I'm having a damn bout of it.

"I'll drink some ginger ale and it'll pass," I assure him. My stomach gurgles, and I groan. "Actually, just go. If I need you, I'll call. The shipyard isn't but ten minutes from here."

He sighs and leans forward to kiss my swollen belly. "I'll be back in an hour. I will make it quick, and Dan will take care of what needs to be done." His hot breath tickles my stomach. "Daddy will be back soon," he tells our baby. Tatiana had asked if we wanted a scan to discover the sex, but we both decided we wanted it to be surprise.

"Be careful," I tell him, my voice cracking with emotion. Lately, I have all of these fears that my husband will die. At the hands of others, a horrific accident, dropping dead of a heart attack. Every terrible way to die, I've thought it. Some nights I can't sleep after having a panic attack over losing him.

He leans forward and kisses my lips. His lips pull up on one side. My body burns with desire every time he looks at me with that sexy smirk of his. "Feed my baby and then I'll come home and feed you."

I laugh and watch him as he crawls out of bed to start dressing. We've been staying at my parent's old house, which now belongs to me, while we stay in the States. Ever since I saw Brie for the first time a couple of weeks ago, we've visited just about each day. I didn't realize how much I missed her. Ren and Calder and Luci are a packaged deal. It's nice having them in my life. And I even got to meet War and Baylee. War was the favor Diego called in several months ago. He acquired some earrings that were fit with a tracking device. It was how they found me in that shipping container.

"Bring back those yummy buffalo wings from that pizza place down the street," I order. When he lifts a brow, I flash him a sweet smile. "Please, Daddy."

He shakes his head. "So demanding, mi diablita."

I shrug and stare at his ass as he bends over to grab some socks from a drawer. "I thought you like it when I get all feisty."

"Feisty for my cock," he corrects and then looks over his shoulder to give me a smoldering grin.

If he weren't about to leave, I'd beg him to stay. I'll show him feisty…

But then another wave of nausea ripples through me. I don't even realize I've closed my eyes until I reopen them and see Diego squatted in front of me beside the bed. Concern has chased away all playfulness in his features.

"I should stay," he murmurs, his thumb dragging along my jaw.

I reach forward and touch his lips. "Go. I'll sleep. When you get back, you can take care of me for the rest of the day."

He stares for a long moment but then gives me a clipped nod. His lips press to mine before he stands upright. "Thirty minutes tops. Sleep."

When the bedroom door clicks shut, I drift off to sleep with my husband as the star of my dirty dreams.

Glass.

I jolt awake and find that I'm drenched in sweat. I'm about to sit up and yank off the T-shirt I'm wearing when I hear heavy footsteps pounding down the hallway. Something about the urgency in the steps tells me my visitor is not Diego.

Shit.

He warned me months ago. The cartel is a dangerous business. Just because we're in love and happy doesn't mean that we aren't still in the thick of the most dangerous criminals in the world. We must always be vigilant and aware. And despite always having men on guard, things can still happen. People can still slip through.

The door flings open and crashes into the wall behind it. I'm stunned frozen when the figure enters the room. The monster before me is horrific. Straight from a nightmare. I am wondering how he came back from the dead just as he speaks.

"Hello, Vee," he snarls, a shiny metal gun in his grip.

I can't help but gape at his disfigured face. Oscar was once so handsome. The sexiest man I knew. But then he lost himself. He turned into this thing. And that was all before his brother bashed his face in. His nose is severely crooked. One of his eyes doesn't open all the way and the eyeball seems to drift. He's baring his teeth at me. Most are broken. The dark hair that he used to wear in a stylish way is bushy and hangs in his face.

"Oscar," I murmur. "What are you doing here? I thought...Esteban... You were so close to death..."

He growls, and the sound sends a shiver up my spine. "After he left with you, I got the hell out of there."

What?

It makes me wonder whose body they threw in with Esteban. Diego told his men to obtain Oscar from the office. Apparently they grabbed the wrong dead guy along the way.

"Why are you here?" I try again. I'm attempting to distract him with words while I work out a plan to defend my baby and myself from this monster.

"You know why I'm here," he hisses. "I'm here to fuck you up like you made my own goddamned brother fuck me up. Then, I'm going to tear your ass up before I put a bullet in your skull."

He yanks the blanket off me, and I scream. His eyes peruse my bare legs but when his gaze finds my rounded belly, he glares.

"I'm pregnant, Oscar," I tell him softly. "Just go. Nobody has to know you were here."

Our eyes meet. His are hate-filled and lost and full of vengeance. Mine are fierce and violent and full of the need to save my child. One of us won't leave this room today.

"Take off your shirt," he demands. "I want to see what you're hiding under there."

I shake my head. "Please leave." *I'm warning you.*

"Vee," he barks. "Take off your goddamned shirt and let me see your stomach."

Time seems to stand still as I'm reminded of when I was seventeen.

"Show me," Oscar begs, his dark eyebrows scrunched together as he gives me a sad face.

I want to show him more than my fake belly button ring but everything is a mess right now. Daddy says I need to squash my feelings for Oscar because he may end up being the one who is to be married to Brie.

But I don't want to squash anything.

I want him.

Brie left earlier, complaining of a headache, so Oscar and I drank by ourselves. Normally, he's wedged between us on the bed as we flirt and cut up. Now, it's just the two of us. I've been friend-zoned hard with him. But sometimes I wonder, if I wasn't too shy to make the first move, could things change between us?

"Show me," he pleads again. His palm rests on my bare thigh. Despite it being an innocent touch, I can't help but tremble from the sensation. His fingers inch up under my cocktail dress, sending ripples of excitement coursing through me.

"I don't think your girlfriend would like me showing you,"

I snip. I've been trying to play hard to get, a new tactic, but I'll be damned if that isn't hard as hell.

"You know I don't have any girlfriends. There are only two girl friends I love." He gives me a lopsided sexy grin that turns my insides to mush.

"Okay," I breathe.

His eyes darken as he grips the bottom of my dress. He drags the silky material up my thighs over my panties. Our gaze is broken when he darts his eyes to look at my panties. When his palm brushes over my pubic bone, I shiver. He palms my stomach and then runs his thumb over the piece of metal that just pinches my skin versus actually piercing it. I bravely reach forward and pull my dress up to just under my breasts to expose my entire stomach to him. The liquor we'd downed earlier does nothing to calm my nerves.

"Vee," he murmurs as he leans forward. "I like it."

I exhale a sharp breath when he kisses my stomach. So innocent yet so full of intent. This could happen. I could finally have Oscar. My panties are wet with excitement. I squirm in need for his touch, but he seems unaware.

"Any other fake piercings I should know about?" he questions, his finger brushing over my clit through my panties.

I jolt and let out a whimper. Say, yes, Vee. "No."

He frowns. "Too bad."

I'm mentally berating myself for being a wussy when his mouth finds my belly button. His teeth latch on to the metal and he tugs on it. It pulls my skin but breaks loose. Our eyes meet for a heated moment, and I know that if we keep flirting at the rate we're going, we're going to have sex. The thought thrills me.

His hand grips the top of my panties just as someone

knocks on the door. I shove my dress down quickly and he sits up. "Who is it?"

"*You're being summoned,*" *Esteban grumbles from the other side of the door.*

Oscar groans and climbs off the bed, a giant boner in his slacks. So close. So damn close. He flashes me a guilty smile before answering the door.

Esteban glances over Oscar's shoulder at me on the bed and smirks. "Two naughty kids up to naughty deeds. Need someone to show you how things work?" He makes a vulgar motion of his finger going in a hole. "I could perform an example, little Oz."

Oscar punches him in the arm. "Shut up. We were just talking. Like always. Friends, fucker."

Esteban snorts and winks at me. "Tell her that."

"Vee." The voice is cold and it drags me out of my warm memory. This man—this monster—is not the boy from my past. That boy died a long time ago. Probably not long after his brother Duvan.

"I always loved you," I murmur, my voice tight with emotion. "I loved you from the moment I walked into your kitchen and you told me to chase after you. I've chased you ever since."

He growls. "I was always here."

"And so was I until…" *You raped me.* I sniffle and shake my head. "Doesn't matter. We weren't meant to be."

His hand shakes but he keeps his weapon pointed at me.

"I miss those days."

A tear leaks out, and I slide my hand under the pillow to grip the cold metal Diego gave me for emergencies. This constitutes as an emergency. "So do I."

"We can't ever get them back, can we?" His voice cracks. The sadness nearly splits me in two.

"No," I whisper. "We can't. Not ever."

A harsh sob catches in his throat. "But I want them. I want them back."

"Oscar, you should leave." Don't make me do this...

His lip trembles. "I don't want to be this person."

"So don't be," I whisper.

He falls to his knees as a gut-wrenching sob escapes him. My heart shatters and breaks. The person who raped me and abused me is long gone. The boy from my past is hurting and lost. I wish I could fix him. I honestly wish I knew how.

"I'm sorry, Vee. I'm so sorry for everything."

He lifts the gun and I panic. I'd been focused on his words, not readying the weapon under my pillow. I stare in horror as the gun slides into his mouth, rather than to point at me. Tears stream down his cheeks.

"Oscar!"

Pop!

So many times I visualized his death after he hurt me. So many times I planned on making him pay. But then...then he broke down in front of me. I didn't see the monster, I saw him. Oscar. Playful, funny, flirtatious Oscar.

A loud sob pierces the air, and I realize it's me. When I scramble to the floor, I know he's gone. Half of his skull is blown out on the wall in front of me. Blood pools on the carpet beneath his head.

I know he's dead.

Yet, I pull him into my arms and hug him anyway.

I tell him everything's going to be okay. That I forgive him. That I love him.

"R-Remember that time we found that p-puppy one summer and we hid him in the woods b-behind your house?" I question through my tears as I hold him to me. "Savvy was her name. She was so cute. How old were we? Eight and Nine?"

He doesn't answer.

He'll never answer again.

"She'd gotten loose from the rope one day and had run away. We both cried so much our dads thought something bad had happened." I laugh and stroke the side of his face. "Your dad kept asking us to give him a name. All we could get out was Savvy. How long did he search for 'the mother-fucker who hurt his kid named Savvy' anyway?"

I lie him back and take his hand in mine. I try not to look at his mangled face or messed up head. Instead, I kiss his knuckles and pretend we're kids again. I'm not sure how long I clutch him, but I'm brought out of my daze when two strong arms lift me. I'm carried like a child into the giant bathroom that used to be my parents. My hero sets me down on the counter before starting the bath. Then, he peels the bloodstained shirt from my body and undresses himself. Carefully, he helps me into the tub and settles behind me.

"What happened, mi amor?" Diego murmurs, his mouth pressing kisses against the back of my head.

I sob and shudder in his arms. "He said he was sorry."

He hugs me tight and doesn't let go.

I hope he never lets go.

XIX | Diego

Several months later...

"I'M A FOOL," I GROWL AS I SPEAR MY FINGERS THROUGH my hair and pace my office.

Jorge laughs—fucking laughs—that asshole. "Never said you weren't."

"How could I do this? How could I let this happen?" I snag my still lit cigar—pink of all fucking colors and straight-up shitty quality—from the ashtray and inhale a big puff.

"Well, everyone knows you think with your cock, man," he snorts.

I glare at him and snub out the abomination in the ashtray. "This is fucked up. I'm a fucked-up person. Karma, hermano. Karma. I have a shitload coming my way."

He smirks. "Why? Because you had five wives at once?" Fucking prick knows how to goad me.

"YES!" I roar.

He stands and dusts off his jacket even though it's in pristine condition. Then he reaches inside to pull out his Glock. "See this?"

I arch a brow at him. "Fuck yeah."

"There are hundreds more where this came from. And just as many badass motherfuckers who will be holding them."

"Your point," I grumble.

"They touch her, they die. Simple."

Some tension eases from my chest. "Simple."

"Now, can we stop celebrating with these lame-ass cigars Tatiana bought and go see this princess I'm going to have to help guard until the day I die?" He grins at me.

I smirk and shake my head. "Let's go see the princess."

She's gorgeous. I'm blown away by how she can look like two people at once. Mine.

"I love that look," Vienna murmurs from our bed, a soft smile on her face. Not four hours ago, she gave birth in her old room to our daughter, Valentina Martina Gomez.

"What look?"

"That one right there. The way you look at her. As if she's your entire world."

I kiss the sweet baby's forehead. "She's not my entire world."

Vienna frowns. "Oh."

I smirk. "You're right there with her."

"There's my romantic," she says with a grin. "You should

let her sleep and come lie down with me." Her hand pats the bed beside her.

I stand from the glider we put in our room and gently place our sleeping child into the bassinet. Once I'm sure she's settled, I crawl in beside my wife. I'm afraid to touch her. I watched Tatiana deliver our daughter and some things can't be unseen. The blood. The stitches. I'd been so disturbed once Tatiana placed a bloody Valentina in Vienna's arms that she asked me to leave until she got them all cleaned up. I close my eyes and gently run my hand along her arm. I hope I never have to see that again.

"You're tense, Diego. What's wrong?"

"I don't like seeing you in pain," I admit and kiss her temple.

"It was worth it," she tells me in a fierce tone.

It's then I know that my brave wife could handle anything, especially childbirth. She's hell on heels with her flaming red hair and fiery spirit. The bastards who wrong her suffer under her iron fist. Just ask Esteban...he knows first hand.

"It was worth it," I agree.

"Everything..."

"Completely."

She turns her head to gaze up at me. I drop a kiss on her forehead and then her nose. And then her sweet, pouty mouth.

"I love you, mi diablita," I murmur.

"I love you too, mi motherfucker."

We both grin.

And then I kiss her again.

And again.

And again.
And again.
And again.
And again until the end.

EPILOGUE | Gabe

I WAKE WITH A START. SOMETHING HEAVY SITS ON MY chest in the darkness. My arms are pinned beneath the weight, and for a split second, I almost toss it off of me. But then I feel her palms on my chest. Exploring. Soft and gentle.

"Why are you awake in the middle of the night, baby?" I murmur as I slide my arms out to grip her hips.

"I've been thinking." Her voice is a whisper. A scary-as-fuck whisper. I hate those goddamned whispers.

"Toto and Land?"

"Sleeping," she assures me. Her fingers brush along my beard in the darkness. "Can we talk?"

I swallow down the tension building inside me. "Of course, angel."

Angel, my ass.

Hannah eats angels for dinner.

But when she's in a mood, I placate her at any cost. I know this. Her parents and brothers know this. Our kids even know this.

She slides off my lap and turns on the bedside lamp. Her blonde hair is messy and wild, but it's her eyes that are distant. So dark. Fuck.

"Talk, beautiful."

The darkness flickers in her eyes as she beams at me. My sweet girl never lets a compliment go. She fucking loves them.

"The medicine doesn't work anymore," she tells me, a slight wobble to her bottom lip. "I think those…things. The bad things."

I jolt upright and reach for her wrist. When I pull her into my arms, she sags against me.

"We'll find something different. Your dad is always researching meds for you." I kiss her tit through her thin nightshirt and then bite it. Sometimes I can distract her from her dark thoughts with sex.

"But what if nothing works. We need a plan."

I stiffen at her words. "A plan for what?"

"Sometimes I stare at them at night. I don't feel like they belong to me. I think terrible things, but then I leave. I'm strong enough to leave." Her voice cracks. "But what happens when one day I'm not?"

Fuck. Fuck. Fuck.

"You're the strongest girl I know," I tell her, squeezing her tight. "Maybe you just need a vacation, baby. You're a good mom. You keep the house in perfect shape and you're a great cook. But you might be working too hard. Why don't we go on a vacation? We'll ask War and Baylee to watch the kids."

She seems to mull over my answer, and I pounce. I peel off her tank top and squeeze her tit before sucking on the soft flesh. Her breath catches when I nibble on her.

"Gabe…"

"Shhh," I murmur. "We'll figure it out in the morning. Until then, let me love you."

My words work because her fingers thread into my hair as she straddles me on the edge of the bed. I flip her onto her back and flash her a wolfish grin before I peel her panties and shorts down her thighs. Once my stunning-but-crazy-as-all-fucking-hell wife is naked, I climb off the bed for a necessity on nights like this.

Rope.

She bites on her bottom lip when I come sauntering back to the bed with the nylon rope. Her eyes are hooded as I tie intricate knots around her wrists so that they don't come loose. Then, I tie the end of the rope to the bed frame.

"Spread 'em," I growl.

My good little girl obeys and shows me her pink pussy. I'm going to punish her cunt for what I can't punish her mind for. I slap it hard enough to make her cry out.

"You want my dick stretching out your ass, don't you, sweet girl?"

She nods. "I want you to hurt me."

I slap her cunt again. "Don't worry. I'm going to hurt you real bad tonight."

Her body shudders in response. Distraction is the best thing I can do for her right now.

"Tell me who owns you," I murmur as I lean forward and suck on her clit.

She jolts against her bindings and releases a long moan.

"Tell me," I order.

When she doesn't answer, I bite her clit hard enough to make her scream out a string of cuss words at me.

"Tell me, goddammit," I snarl against her wet cunt.

"Y-You. You always have."

"Good girl." I kiss her pussy softly. As I take my time teasing her, my brain is elsewhere. This shit gets worse every day. The meds don't work. Nothing fucking works. It scares the hell out of me the way she looks at our children.

Fuck. Fuck. Fuck.

"Mmmmm," she moans.

"That's it, sweet girl. Come for me and then I'll put my dick inside you. If you're a real good girl, I might put it in your ass later, too."

My words turn her on because she whimpers as her orgasm nears. I suck on her swollen clit until she cries out in pleasure. Her entire body trembles, but I don't give her time to recover. I shove my boxers down and flop my hard cock out. I'm always hard for my sweet girl.

"Oh, Hannah," I growl as I thrust hard inside her tight cunt. I lean over her and find her perfect mouth. Our kiss is needy and hungry and unhinged—like our entire relationship. Fucking hell, it's perfect.

But it's *not* perfect because when she's not tied to my bed, letting me fuck her, she's on a train by herself riding full speed ahead to crazy town. And she's going to mow down my family in the process.

"God, I fucking love you," I tell her with a grunt.

She whimpers and sucks on my tongue. "I fucking love you, too."

I pound into her until we're both moaning with our release. I come deep inside her cunt because my shit is fixed. No more babies with my hot ass wife. I can barely protect the two we've got.

I grin as I look deep into her blue eyes that have found clarity again. Love shines in them. It's real and genuine.

For now.

With a stifled sigh, I stroke her hair and memorize her face.

One day, I won't see this look in her eyes anymore.

One day, I'm going to have to kill my wife.

Not THE END.

But it will be soon.

The final installment of the *War & Peace* series

is on its way…

This is the End, Baby
(epilogue novella)

PLAYLIST

Listen on Spotify

"Paper Planes" by M.I.A.

"Fuck With Myself" by Banks

"Weaker Girl" by Banks

"Desire" by Meg Myers

"I Really Want You to Hate Me" by Meg Myers

"Royals" by Lorde

"Heads Will Roll" by Yeah Yeah Yeahs

"Not Afraid Anymore" by Halsey

"#1 Crush" by Garbage

"Dark Nights" by Dorothy

"Zombie" by The Cranberries

"Going to Hell" by The Pretty Reckless

"I Put a Spell on You" by Annie Lennox

"Criminal" by Fiona Apple

"Fade Into You" by Mazzy Star

"Dog Days Are Over" by Florence + The Machine

"Tear In My Heart" by Twenty One Pilots

"Ride" by Twenty One Pilots

"S&M" by Rihanna

"The Monster" by Eminem

"Everybody Wants to Rule the World" by Lorde

"Elastic Heart" by Sia

"The Devil Within" by Digital Daggers

"Bloodstream" by Stateless

"Cough Syrup" by Young the Giant

"Blood in the Cut" by K. Flay

"Is She With You?" by Hans Zimmer

"Uprising" by Muse

"Bad Girls" by M.I.A.

"River" by Bishop Briggs

"Are You Alone Now?" by Dead Sea Empire

"Castle" by Halsey

Books by K Webster

The Breaking the Rules Series:
Broken (Book 1)
Wrong (Book 2)
Scarred (Book 3)
Mistake (Book 4)
Crushed (Book 5 – a novella)

The Vegas Aces Series:
Rock Country (Book 1)
Rock Heart (Book 2)
Rock Bottom (Book 3)

The Becoming Her Series:
Becoming Lady Thomas (Book 1)
Becoming Countess Dumont (Book 2)
Becoming Mrs. Benedict (Book 3)

War & Peace Series:
This is War, Baby (Book 1)
This is Love, Baby (Book 2)
This Isn't Over, Baby (Book 3)
This Isn't You, Baby (Book 4)
This is Me, Baby (Book 5)
This Isn't Fair, Baby (Book 6)

2 Lovers Series:
Text 2 Lovers (Book 1)
Hate 2 Lovers (Book 2)

Alpha & Omega Duet:
Alpha & Omega (Book 1)
Omega & Love (Book 2)

Pretty Stolen Dolls Duet:
Pretty Stolen Dolls (Book 1)
Pretty Lost Dolls (Book 2)

Taboo Treats:
Bad Bad Bad

Standalone Novels:
Apartment 2B
Love and Law
Moth to a Flame
Erased
The Road Back to Us
Surviving Harley
Give Me Yesterday
Running Free
Dirty Ugly Toy
Zeke's Eden
Sweet Jayne
Untimely You
Mad Sea
Whispers and the Roars
Schooled by a Senior
B-Sides and Rarities
Blue Hill Blood by Elizabeth Gray

ACKNOWLEDGEMENTS

Thank you to my husband…you're always an inspiration and I love you so much!

A huge thank you to my Krazy for K Webster's Books reader group. You all are insanely supportive and I can't thank you enough.

A gigantic thank you to my betas who read this story. Elizabeth Clinton, Ella Stewart, Shannon Miller, Amy Bosica, Brooklyn Miller, Robin Martin, Amy Simms, Jessica Viteri, Amanda Söderlund, and Jessica Hollyfield, you all helped make this story even better. Your feedback and early reading is important to this entire process and I can't thank you enough.

Also, a big thank you to Vanessa Renee Place for proofreading this story!! Love you!

A big thank you to my author friends who have given me your friendship and your support. You have no idea how much that means to me.

Thank you to all of my blogger friends both big and small that go above and beyond to always share my stuff. You all rock! #AllBlogsMatter

I am totally thankful for my author group, the COPA gals, for being there when I need to take a load off and whine. Y'all rock!

Vanessa with Prema Editing, thanks so much for editing this book! You rock! Your love for this series is important to the finished product! Also a huge thank you to Jessica Descent for being second set of eyes!

Thank you Stacey Blake for being a super star as always

when formatting my books and in general. I love you! I love you! I love you!

A big thanks to my PR gal, Nicole Blanchard. You are fabulous at what you do and keep me on track!

Lastly but certainly not least of all, thank you to all of the wonderful readers out there that are willing to hear my story and enjoy my characters like I do. It means the world to me!

ABOUT THE AUTHOR

K Webster is the author of dozens of romance books in many different genres including contemporary romance, historical romance, paranormal romance, dark romance, romantic suspense, and erotic romance. When not spending time with her hilarious and handsome husband and two adorable children, she's active on social media connecting with her readers.

Her other passions besides writing include reading and graphic design. K can always be found in front of her computer chasing her next idea and taking action. She looks forward to the day when she will see one of her titles on the big screen.

Join K Webster's newsletter to receive a couple of updates a month on new releases and exclusive content. To join, all you need to do is go to
http://authorkwebster.us10.list-manage.com/subscribfe?u=36473e274a1bf9597b508ea72&id=96366b-b08e).

Facebook: www.facebook.com/authorkwebster

Blog: authorkwebster.wordpress.com/

Twitter:twitter.com/KristiWebster

Email: kristi@authorkwebster.com

Goodreads: www.goodreads.com/user/show/10439773-k-webster

Instagram: instagram.com/kristiwebster